"How on earth did that compel you to come here and try to talk me into starting this fling we're supposed to have?"

Slipping his hand to her nape, Mack drew her toward him. "I admit it defies logic. But while it would probably be smarter for me to leave you alone, that is one empty and ugly house without you in it."

With that he closed his lips over hers. There wasn't any anger or frustration this time. He simply wanted to make sure that she thought of him after he left. He sure as hell would be thinking of her.

He liked how she let him direct the kiss, liked realizing that her lips felt even better than he remembered, and how her tongue accepted then flirted with his. He groaned, wanting to unbutton her uniform and begin to learn what else she liked.

When he finally, reluctantly, eased his lips from hers, he found her slow to open her eyes. Feeling a tug somewhere deep inside, he kissed one eyelid, then the other.

"How sweet," she murmured, sounding touched. "Didn't know you had that in you."

"Don't let it get around."

Dear Reader,

Although scientists like to debunk the idea that blue moons are anything other than a mathematical phenomenon, they remain rare enough to be special and romantic to some of us. It proves life-changing to Alana Anders and Mack Graves one night in August while under a bright, full, *blue* moon in Oak Grove, Texas. On the surface, Officer Anders seems to bear an old family tragedy well enough, and Mack—just retired from the Marine Corps—hopes to mend fences with his long-estranged father as he recovers from wounds suffered in Afghanistan. But as is often the case, there's a great deal more going on beneath the surface with these two. I hope you will enjoy their journey of the heart.

While there was a community called Oak Grove in Wood County, Texas (established in the 1850s, with businesses active through the 1930s), all the stores are long gone and only a few houses remain. My Oak Grove is fictitious.

I do hope you'll enjoy Alana and Mack's time in Memphis, where they stay at the famous Peabody Hotel. I was a few days premature with Chez Philippe's autumn menu, but the dinner described was reflective of what is served.

Thanks, always, for being a reader, and please check out my website at HelenRMyers.com, or look for me on Facebook under Helen Myers.

With warm regards,

Helen

A HOLIDAY TO REMEMBER

HELEN R. MYERS

HARLEQUIN®

entertain, enrich, inspire™

ISBN-13: 978-0-373-65707-0

A HOLIDAY TO REMEMBER

Books by Helen R. Myers

Harlequin Special Edition

It's News to Her #2130
Almost a Hometown Bride #2171
The Surprise of Her Life #2190
A Holiday to Remember #2225

Silhouette Special Edition

After That Night... #1066
Beloved Mercenary #1162
What Should Have Been #1758
A Man to Count On #1830
The Last Man She'd Marry #1914
Daddy on Demand #2004
Hope's Child #2045
It Started with a House... #2070

Silhouette Romance

Confidentially Yours #677
Invitation to a Wedding #737
A Fine Arrangement #776
Through My Eyes #814
Three Little Chaperones #861
Forbidden Passion #908
A Father's Promise #1002
To Wed at Christmas #1049
The Merry Matchmaker #1121
Baby in a Basket #1169

Silhouette Books

Silhouette Shadows Collection 1992
 "Seawitch"

Montana Mavericks
 The Law Is No Lady

Silhouette Desire

The Pirate O'Keefe #506
Kiss Me Kate #570
After You #599
When Gabriel Called #650
Navarrone #738
Jake #797
Once upon a Full Moon #857
The Rebel and the Hero #941
Just a Memory Away #990
The Officer and the Renegade #1102

Silhouette Shadows

Night Mist #6
Whispers in the Woods #23
Watching for Willa #49

Harlequin MIRA

Come Sundown
More Than You Know
Lost
Dead End
Final Stand
No Sanctuary
While Others Sleep

Other titles by this author
available in ebook format.

HELEN R. MYERS

is a collector of two- and four-legged strays, and lives deep in the Piney Woods of East Texas. She cites cello music and bonsai gardening as favorite relaxation pastimes, and still edits in her sleep—an accident, learned while writing her first book. A bestselling author of diverse themes and focus, she is a three-time RITA® Award nominee, winning for *Navarrone* in 1993.

Chapter One

"Do you think he's a jumper?"

The excited voice on the other end of her police radio had Officer Alana Anders groaning inwardly. All she'd reported was that she'd spotted someone loitering along Oak Grove, Texas's, flooding Miller Creek. How that constituted a 911 crisis was all in dispatcher Barbara Jayne "Bunny" Dodd's vivid imagination.

"Bunny, he's sitting on a tree stump that's no higher than a park bench would be if this town wasn't too cheap to put any in," Alana told the information-addicted woman. "Unless he has a rocket strapped to a part of his anatomy that I can't see, he'd need to be an Olympic long jumper, not a diver, to make the fifteen-to-twenty feet it is to the edge of the water."

It was unusual to see the creek in this condition—especially since there was no hurricane blowing up from the Gulf of Mexico. But there *was* a change in weather patterns going on. It was flooding in Oklahoma and Arkansas; as a result, while East Texas was seeing little in the way of precipitation, the northern counties' tributaries were inheriting a splendid overflow.

"But it's a *blue moon*," her coworker declared, the announcement coming out of nowhere.

An aspiring writer in her free time, the divorcée was chock-full of trivia that most people forgot minutes after hearing it. While Alana sometimes found her prattling a help to stay awake during many an uneventful shift, others avoided the woman exactly because of her wandering focuses of interest as much as her relentless chattiness. She'd certainly knocked one out of the park this time with that blue-moon reference.

"Excuse me?" Alana peered out of her windshield to check the sky in case she was really missing something of astronomical significance.

"They're rare because it takes two to three years to build up on the yearly extra days to have a second full moon in a month. It's said that this August one is among the rarest. That has to mean something."

"Not according to CNN this morning," Alana replied. "They said the scientific world has taken all the mystery out of the event. Supposedly a volcano eruption caused the appearance of a blue moon—and some green sunsets. Krakatoa back in…1883, I think they said. So the other references that go back another couple of hundred years could well have been due to equally logical coincidences. But, hey, if it will make you happy, I'll gladly ask our fellow insomniac if he's a galactic visitor here to correct the last half-dozen mathematical errors in calculating the end of the world. That's our job, right? Leave no question unanswered."

Bunny sighed. "Oh, Ally, you don't usually make fun of me the way the others do. And where's your sense of romance? You like music. You know musicians were referencing the blue moon in song forever."

"And you know that I don't listen to Elvis," Alana replied, feeling the pinch of a tension headache coming on. "Who, by the way, also offered his services to Nixon—or was it J. Edgar—to be an agent for the U.S. Give me a break, Bunny."

"Not just Elvis," Bunny replied in her most little-girl voice. "Mr. Richard Rogers. You like Broadway."

"I like beer and bourbon, too. Unfortunately, I'm on duty." At Bunny's prolonged silence—obviously due to wounded feelings—Alana lifted her gaze to the heavens again. "Okay, okay, I'm going to make an effort… after all, it has been a while since I've had the cheap thrill of frisking a total stranger."

"Now, you stop," the dispatcher demanded. "For all you know, he could be suffering from a broken heart. Maybe he's been somehow led here to be *your* guy."

Alana had heard enough. "Listen, Sherlock—"

"What does he look like?"

"Bunny," Alana said, tone pleading, "I'm too far away from him to tell, and you know the lighting isn't great over here."

"Well, go find out before he goes and does something you might both regret for the rest of your lives."

Alana decided the only thing that she was regretting at the moment was reporting the situation when she did. To heck with procedure, she should have just gone and checked things out, then radioed her findings afterward. "Consider me gone. *You* hold off drafting an engagement announcement for the newspaper until I at least introduce myself, okay?"

"What I am going to do is notify Ed for backup. It's been a while since we've had a stranger come through town."

Now she remembered why they cut her a check every two weeks? "Barbara Jayne Dodd—*cease and desist.*" The woman's mindset could go from softhearted romance writer to police-procedural novelist faster than a career perp could blame someone else for his problems. No wonder she wasn't published yet; she was all over the map with her feelings and focus. A person would have to be schizophrenic to keep up with her.

But Alana did sympathize to a degree. Oak Grove, population 3,900, was a challenge to her, too. The town hierarchy claimed it could barely justify the police force they had—especially around raise time—and yet protected the top tier that officiated over criminal behavior, so that things like drug trafficking and subsequent related crimes couldn't be crushed, only minimally controlled. As a result, Alana was often accused of being an adrenaline junkie herself and just "looking for trouble." That said, she wasn't about to let what was probably a simple 11-94, Pedestrian Stop, get turned into something that could cost the chief another prescription for his ulcer.

"Will you please let Ed have his donut break?" she

told Bunny. "With Sue Ann out of town visiting their daughter and new grandbaby, this is the only time he doesn't get his clothes checked for sugar-glaze crumbs. If I think there's a need to bring him in on this, you'll be the first to know."

Signing off, she exited her white patrol car with the bold red-and-blue writing on the side, and angled south beyond the vehicle a few yards in order not to approach the man from the rear and startle him. As much as she wanted to rein in their dispatcher's imagination, she wasn't about to drop her guard. Aided by the very moon that had Bunny sounding as though a serial Lothario might be on the loose, Alana saw that the man continued to sit quietly, leaning forward to rest his forearms on his knees, staring unblinkingly at the fast-flowing creek. Unless he was deaf, drugged or otherwise hearing impaired, he had to have heard her pull up behind him, and could still hear the patrol car's engine continue to idle.

Usually no more than a dozen feet wide, the creek was now at least twice that. Nevertheless, as she'd attested to Bunny, the stranger was not in harm's way yet; Alana could confirm that from her new vantage point. Also, so far, she didn't think she knew him. He was wearing a dark-colored T-shirt—she was now guessing it was olive-green due to the duffel bag between his feet—jeans and athletic shoes. If he was a drifter, there was nothing shabby about him, and given his buzzed haircut and lean but toned build, her first guess was that he was military, or at least recently discharged. A veteran on his way home? He sure didn't seem in any hurry. With that in mind, she also had to consider the spike in suicide rates due to veterans suffering from post-traumatic stress. Then there was the AWOL possibility, another reason for sticking to back roads and night travel to keep out of sight.

In the mysterious blue-white light of Bunny's moon, his hair color was difficult to define, and the close haircut didn't help. It looked at once ashy, then brown, but not as dark as her own. One thing was for certain: with each step, the closer view of his profile discounted Latino, Native American or Middle Eastern ethnicity. In fact, he could be Kevin Bacon's kid brother.

"Sir? Everything okay here?"

At first the man acted as though he hadn't heard her, but after another few seconds, he rolled his head, chin leading, to inspect the intrusion on his privacy. Was that sweeping glance and subtle shake of his head for a woman being in uniform, for the fact that she'd had the audacity to approach him by herself, or what? Whatever his thinking, he returned his attention to the water.

"Am I breaking some ordinance, *Officer?*"

"Technically, not at all," Alana replied, allowing a touch of humor to enter her voice. "But at this hour, our four-legged scavengers tend to assume that this trail is their territory. If one happens to confront you, I'd strongly advise you to voluntarily surrender any food you're in possession of—especially if it's pizza or hot dogs from the convenience store down the block."

She followed that comment by a nod toward the brightest lights in town. It earned her an "are you for real?" look.

"Here's the thing," Alana said in response to that. She was now confident that she had his full attention and that he wasn't high on something. "It's after one in the morning and it's obvious that you're not here to fish, or throw change into the creek and make a wish. If by chance you have another plan less pleasant, it's my responsibility to convince you to reconsider."

That won her another disbelieving glance.

"Oh, yes, sir, I'm serious," she said, although her tone remained amiable. "And look at that current, the dirty foam against the bank, and the litter accumulating in the tall weeds. No telling what else is in that water. Do you *really* want to deal with an angry woman having to face an admittedly overdue tetanus shot, not to mention getting her hair messed up?"

While his expression said, *You and what crane?* he replied, "I'm not planning anything. I was just taking a break. Thinking. Have politicians figured out a way to put restrictions on that, too?"

"Rumor has it something is tucked away in an upcoming city council bill." But Alana was relieved that the man could form such a coherent sentence. "I don't recognize you as a local."

"I'm not. Well, once. Not anymore."

"So you're passing through to touch bases with someone before heading elsewhere?"

"Probably."

Alana could visualize Bunny scribbling down this dialogue for some work in progress, but she was finding it as enjoyable as scraping lint out of a dryer vent. "What might change your mind?" When he didn't seem to want to answer, Alana tried a different angle. "My institutionally disrespected female intuition is telling me that you're military. Reassure me that you're not AWOL."

"Officer," he enunciated, "I'm retired and the least of anyone's worries."

Ordinarily, that would suffice for her—except for the defeated and world-weary tone in his voice. "I appreciate that, sir. I'm Officer Alana Anders, Oak Grove P.D. And you are?"

It took him a good while, but finally he offered, "Mack."

Alana could start to feel the roots of her hair follicles aching as she mentally visualized pulling them out of her head. "You'll have to do a little better than that."

"Graves."

She had to lock her knees to keep from taking a step back. "Mack Graves." Her heart went into such chaos, she couldn't help but take several deep breaths for the skidding and colliding going on behind her ribs. Especially when she started to see something familiar about his face. "Fred's Mackenzie?"

"Just Mack. Mackenzie is my mother's maiden name and it was hell getting through school with it, let alone dealing with the ridicule in boot camp." The look he added suggested that if she remembered nothing else, she shouldn't forget to avoid calling him that again. "But, yeah, Fred is my father. I angled down this way to see if he wanted to try again in the relationship department. I suspect if you know Fred, you know *warm* and *fuzzy* aren't the first descriptions that come to mind."

Despite her training, Alana momentarily struggled

with deeper emotions, and not only because Mack Graves had used the wrong tense. To her, Fred *had* been those things—although, she would allow, not to everyone.

"You have been away for some time." She wished she could delay telling him the bad news, but she couldn't. "We were trying to find you. I'm sorry to say—so sorry to tell you—that your father passed away last month."

After another long look, the unusually self-contained man nodded once, twice, then simply hung his head and stared at the duffel bag between his feet.

Alana had no problem picking up on the shock and turmoil going on inside him. She knew all about such emotions…and much more.

So the prodigal son had returned. Fred's ex-wife, Dina, had left him years ago—and had taken their eight-year-old boy with her. She had hated small-town living and Fred's iron grip on their finances. Word had it that the boy had returned once, as a teenager during a summer break, but had left soon afterward, never to return. The gossip mill concluded that Fred had been abusive at the worst, and a cold miser at best. At the time, Alana had only started grade school and was preoccupied with horses and flying, the latter a passion her older brother had infected her with, so she had remained blissfully oblivious to all of that. It was only later that she'd come to learn how inaccurate the gossips were. That wasn't to say that Fred hadn't been a disciplinarian, and frugal, but what had he been dealing with in a boy who no longer remembered, let alone respected, him?

"I'm sorry for your loss," she said, hoping he didn't

catch the hitch in her voice that had gone husky. He didn't need to know that the loss of Fred was hard on her, too. "Although I can see the resemblance to your father, I'd appreciate seeing some ID. Then you can come with me to the station. There are papers you need to sign before we hand things over to you."

"He was cremated?"

"Yes, but..." Alana hesitated in telling him everything yet, so she pointed across the street to the city cemetery. "We ended up placing the urn over there. Under the big oak at the northwest corner between his parents, your grandparents. I was talking about the keys to the ranch—house, truck, barn, things like that. You're his sole beneficiary. That's the other reason that we've been trying to locate you."

"I see."

After the slow, enigmatic response, Mack pulled out his billfold and took out his driver's license. Despite her certainty that he was who he claimed to be, Alana still accepted it with her usual caution when dealing with strangers, then used her LED penlight to see that it was a current one from Virginia. The address was an apartment and she would bet anything he no longer considered it home. She also noted that he was born in mid-February, thirty-eight years ago. The photo was clearly the man before her, maybe ten pounds heavier, with fewer signs of life and its stresses. Returning the flashlight to her pocket, she tucked away the ID, as well.

"Okay, I'll hang on to this to make a copy at the station. Grab your bag and let's go. Afterward, I'll drive you out to the ranch."

"You don't have to do that. I guess I remember enough to find it myself."

While he hadn't been out of the service long enough to go soft, on foot a relatively healthy person might make Fred's ranch by the first hint of daylight. Such a trek was neither safe at this hour, nor would it be considerate. "Fred was more than a neighbor and friend," she said, by way of explanation. "He was like family to me. It's the least I can do."

As Mack Graves put his duffel bag in the backseat of the patrol car and eased into the passenger side, Alana settled in the driver's seat. "Which branch were you in?"

"Marines."

Then he could definitely make the hike faster than most people, but she still wasn't going to allow that. "Were you in Iraq or Afghanistan?"

"Both."

Whoa, Alana thought. "Glad you made it back—and in one piece."

He turned away to look out the passenger window, but she took no offense; after all, she had just given him some life-altering news. What's more, not everyone appreciated the "thank you for your service" attitude. She'd concluded more that some just wanted to fulfill their obligation and get on with their lives. On the other hand, a simple "Thanks" in return wouldn't rupture his spleen.

"I'm not trying to be chatty."

"I'm glad to hear that."

Lifting her eyebrows at the borderline-rude response, Alana knew there was no way she was going to be quiet and circumspect now. "Ah. You're the strong, silent type. Then you'd better prepare yourself for Bunny. She's our night-shift dispatcher. I'm quite shy, in comparison. In fact, I became a cop to force myself to be more outgoing."

She felt his sidelong look, but kept her eyes on the road. None of what she'd said was accurate, but she didn't care. He'd made up his mind about her from the moment she approached him, and it irked that the news about Fred hadn't softened his edges one bit.

"Doesn't your family worry when you go out playing commando after dark?"

There it was, Alana thought with a wry twist of her lips. The derision she'd felt from him at first glance. But if he thought he was going to make her cower, he'd misjudged her more than he could imagine.

"I don't see any part of being a cop as playing," she replied, maintaining her pleasant tone. "Security checks on strangers in the park included. And as far as family is concerned, Uncle Duke is it, all two-hundred-fifty pounds, six feet four of him. Since he's the chief of police, and before that was a state trooper, and before that a marine himself, if he didn't feel that I'd been fully trained to do my job, I wouldn't be sitting here talking to you right now."

Mack's soft groan and the way he dropped his head against the headrest had her lips curling into a satisfied smile.

What she failed to add to all that was that Duke hated that she'd become a police officer and had been doing his best to marry her off or otherwise get her off the force from her first day on the job. The only thing that helped keep him semiquiet about it was the knowledge that if he didn't allow her to be a member of their hometown department, she would go elsewhere...or take on a career that was even more demanding and dangerous.

"Don't worry, gyrene," she drawled, using the marines' favorite expression for themselves. Uncle Duke had told her about how it had evolved back in World War II. The hard-fighting U.S. soldiers had been dubbed GIs, but marines considered themselves tougher yet, and wanted to be called marines. So the term *GI and marine* became *gyrene*. "You're not in trouble with him... or me, for that matter. Attitudes like yours are as common as scales on a fish."

She pulled into the station located on the other side of the cemetery—barely a half mile from the park. Parking by the front sidewalk in the otherwise-empty lot, she invited Mack to keep his duffel bag where it was, then she escorted him inside.

"Ally—darn it!" Bunny declared the second they came through the door. "You turned off your radio, didn't you? And you didn't radio back. I was about to call Ed even though you said not to."

The strawberry-blonde with the corkscrew curls and baby voice leaped to her feet exposing more of a zaftig body stuffed in a half-size-too-small blue shirt and jeans. It was a good try at claiming indignation, but Alana knew the divorcée, who served as a civilian clerk and dispatcher, had already spotted Mack and was really showing off her five-foot-two frame in case he wasn't into "brunette amazons," as she'd dubbed her.

"Buns, the door was unlocked" was all Alana said to the woman who was six years her senior. But the look she sent her reminded her of department policy when no "badges" were on the premises.

"Ally." Bunny shot her a look that went from withering to pleading before offering Mack a dimpled smile. "Is everything okay?"

"Everything is fine," Alana intoned. Then she added evenly, "This is Mack Graves, Fred's son."

"Oh! Aw." Bunny's big, brown calf eyes went soft with sympathy. "Condolences for your loss."

"Our dispatcher, Barbara Jayne Dodd," Alana told Mack with a wave. To Bunny, she continued, "We're going to take care of some paperwork. Then I'm taking him up to the ranch. *Now* you can call Ed. Tell him that I expect to be back in about a half hour. *Only* Ed," Alana added. "Let's assure Mr. Graves at least one night of peace before the press and the gossip hounds start salivating."

"Yes, ma'am."

Fluorescent lighting wasn't complimentary to anyone, but when Alana led Mack to her desk at the far corner of the room and finally faced him, she saw how gaunt he looked, and wondered if he wasn't dehydrated, as well as in need of food. "Can I offer you a soda? Water? Coffee? When did you last eat?"

"I'm fine."

"I appreciate that you'd like to get out of here, pronto, and be alone again, but while the refrigerator at your house is running, the contents are wanting—unless you're into condiments. I should add that the supermarket doesn't reopen until six o'clock. We can stop at the twenty-four-hour convenience store, even if the selection is iffy and ridiculously expensive, or we can stop at our place, which is actually next door to Last Call. If you like, I can fix you up with a few essentials to get you through the next day or two."

"I take it that's where your uncle—the chief—is?" At her nod, Mack shook his head. "Far be it from me to disrupt his sleep."

"Smart decision," she replied with a cheeky grin. "But that means you're getting either a cola with all the sugar, or coffee with creamer and sweetener. Pick your poison."

"Coffee."

"Good choice. It's my machine and great stuff. No blending nonsense, powdered milk or artificial sweeteners. Sit tight." With a smart turn on her heel that sent her ponytail swinging, she went to get it. She was acutely aware of his narrow-eyed stare all the while she worked, and when she returned, she set the big mug before him, then took a power bar from her center desk drawer, and slid it at him. "Here, that will help, too."

"Are you always this bossy?"

"You'll have to try harder than that to get under this skin, gyrene," she countered, all pleasantness. "The truth is that I'm nowhere near the sweetheart Bunny is, but kids and stray animals do tend to cling to me like Velcro. Go figure."

Mack Graves glanced up from stirring his coffee to eye her from beneath dense lashes a shade darker than his hair. In the bright light, Alana finally saw that his eyes were an odd green-gray, the shade of Southern moss. She'd never seen anyone with that coloring before and quickly reached for the rubber-banded bulky envelope in the bottom drawer of her desk.

"Here we are," she said, setting it on her blotter. "I have a number of keys, copies of his death certificate, and his will. As I said, you're his sole beneficiary. One thing l need to remind you of—in case you're not aware of it—is that in Texas there's a ninety-day survivorship clause before you can probate his estate, so I hope you're planning to stick around."

"I wasn't."

His answer didn't surprise Alana. Fred had spoken of his son enough to worry about ever finding him, let alone passing on all this responsibility. But she'd made promises. Slipping out a single sheet that declared he was accepting possession of the package, she marked an X where she wanted Mack to sign, then slid it over to him.

She placed the pen on top as a precursor to what she was about to say.

"I hope you'll rethink that. Oak Grove may be a small town in the middle of dozens of small, even dying, towns, but Last Call is a wonderful place. On the other hand, if you want to sell it, I'm sure there are several people who would make you an offer soon enough. The property continues to be on a paved farm-to-market road. Fred was a fine fence builder, and the pastures are some of the best in the county. Our two properties share a creek, but more importantly, the darned place sits on an aquifer and there are three deep wells to keep ponds full regardless of the weather trends. Fred wasn't as particular about the house, but what it lacks in style, it makes up for in sturdiness. As for the barn, it's big enough to protect the machinery from the elements and to store feed. Behind it are the horse stables. There are only two horses these days—Fred's mount, Rooster, who's pretty old and is kept as a pet, and Eberardo's horse, Blanco. The rest of the pens are used to tend to injured or orphaned stock."

"Do you sell real estate during the day?"

Understanding what he was insinuating, Alana shrugged. "Yeah, I'm kind of attached to the place, as I am to my own home." Remembering something, Alana glanced at her watch, which read nearly two in the morning—winced—and reached for her phone. "Eberardo Chavez is the hand who still lives on the property. You'll see his trailer on the side of the barn and sheds. I'm going to call him to let him know not to worry if he sees me pull in and the house light up. More likely, Two Dog would announce our arrival as soon as the front gate opens."

"Who the hell is that?"

"Eberardo's dog. His second dog since working at Last Call. He's a good man and hard worker, but he's no cowboy poet."

Moments later, she heard Eberardo's groggy voice.

"*Sí,* Señorita Ally. *¿Es todo lo correcto?*"

Aware that he had caller ID, Alana replied, "*Lo siento.* Sorry to disturb you, Eberardo. Everything is fine. I just wanted you to know that Two Dog may start

barking shortly, and you might see lights at the house.
I'm letting Mr. Fred's son, Mack, in."

"Ah, he has come. Mr. Fred would be much happy."

"Pienso tan, también," Ally replied, telling him that
she thought so, too. "We'll talk more tomorrow. Go
back to sleep."

"To happy dreams. We wait for this day, eh? *Gracias,* Señorita Ally."

As Alana disconnected, hoping he was right, she saw
Mack pick up the pen and scrawl his signature across
the bottom of the paper. When finished, he pushed it
and the pen back toward her. Finally, he took a tenta-
tive sip of coffee, followed by a more appreciative gulp.

"Anything else?" he asked.

"You can admit it's good coffee," she said, amuse-
ment and challenge in her gaze.

"Why waste my breath telling you what you already
know?"

He was Fred's son all right, Alana thought. Mule-
headed, confident and all man with those penetrating
eyes letting a woman know that no matter what, sex
was always in the mindset. She shoved the paper into
the top drawer of her desk and handed over the banded
bundle. "You can take the coffee and protein bar with
you. Consider the mug a housewarming gift."

Minutes later, back at the patrol car, Mack gingerly
took his seat. As he fastened his seat belt, he tried to
ignore Alana's open stare.

"You okay?"

"Yeah, why?"

"You're moving like someone ten or fifteen years older than you are."

"Hitching and hiking can do that to you."

Alana seemed to accept that and exited the parking lot. She turned onto Main Street for the turn north that would take them to the farm-to-market road and Last Call Ranch. In all honesty, that's all Mack remembered of the directions to the place. But his back hurt so much from carrying the duffel bag—even though he changed shoulders frequently—that he mentally kissed her for insisting on driving him. At least none of his wounds had busted open. He'd fingered the spots when she'd gone to get him coffee.

The town was literally ghostlike with not another vehicle in sight, until he caught a glimpse of lights and spotted a patrol car in his side-view mirror as it left the convenience store and turned toward the station. No doubt the other night-shift cop, Ed, coming to catch up on the excitement with dispatcher Bunny.

Buns, he thought with a silent snort, remembering Alana's personal nickname for her. The woman had certainly earned that one, too, although she seemed pretty harmless and sweet—and again, all wrong for a police station. And how the devil did females sit for hours in clothes that tight without losing consciousness? But at least she wasn't in a uniform.

Mack had never cared for the idea of women in uniform, although he'd had his butt saved twice by female chopper pilots and had since adjusted his opinion to a degree. However, he wasn't changing his mind about Alana Anders. Maybe she seemed to know what she was doing, but she was too feminine, too much woman for what she did for a living. That annoyed him as much as it did to realize that his gaze was drawn to her whenever he thought she wasn't looking.

Face it, you don't care if she's noticing or not.

Fine, he amended, if things were different, he would be coming after her, staking his claim like the red-blooded male he was. He may have been shot twice, but as far as he could tell, all of his equipment still worked, and he was going to prove that as soon as he regained a little more strength. In the meantime, he was going to dream about Officer Anders's long legs out of those uniform blues. He would bet a month's pay that she had the legs of a swimsuit model and that her breasts weren't filled with silicone. That face could be on a magazine cover, too, but the fools would want to airbrush away the small scar above her left eyebrow, and put too much greasy stuff on those succulent lips. He would like to taste them wet from a bite of strawberry or a lush peach, as he lost himself in those deceptively soft brown eyes.

Nuts, he thought.

Deceptive was the key word. There was a lot going on inside her and he wasn't sure of a fraction of it. One minute she was all business, the next she was giving him a look so honest and bold, he felt as though he'd taken an electric shock to his groin, and the next he could swear her heart was fracturing. What the hell was going on with her?

At least it seemed that she'd been decent to the old man. Mack thought his father had been a lucky stiff if he'd checked out while gazing at Alana's high-cheekboned face, especially if that luscious hair wasn't tied back as it was now.

"How long have you been at this?" They were at least a mile outside town, and security lights were growing fewer and farther between, and Mack figured her mind was cranking away questions, too. He'd rather have her answering than asking them.

"You mean law enforcement? I went into the academy straight from college."

"So you're a rookie?" He suspected she was slightly older than that, but not by much.

"Hilarious. This is my seventh year. I just turned thirty."

Mentally, he gave her another point for being honest. At thirty, some women started counting backward. "So this is really what you always wanted to do?"

"You didn't hear me say that. I wanted to be a fighter pilot. I caught the flying bug from my older brother. He would be your age now."

"Would be?"

"He was flying my parents to the Gulf to catch a cruise for their twentieth wedding anniversary, but there was mechanical trouble. They didn't make it."

"That's rough." She'd managed to keep her voice steady, but Mack didn't miss how her hands worked the steering wheel and how tight her grip got.

"It was. Is. But coming back to the world, as you service people tend to say, has to be a challenge, too." Alana's voice grew huskier. "And then to have this news that you weren't expecting…"

She didn't really want to talk about the past any more

than he did. That was another thing he couldn't help but find appealing about her. He'd OD'd on drama queens years before finally freeing himself of his mother. "I am curious as to why my father didn't hire an attorney to handle this," he said, shifting the envelope between his hands.

"His longtime lawyer passed away last year and he didn't like the other two in town. I tried to help him find someone else, but he kept putting it off until it was too late."

"So his death wasn't sudden?"

"No, there's nothing fast about lung cancer." Alana shook her head as though trying to shake off something. "He never could quit smoking. Heaven knows, we all tried to help."

"He'd known you all of your life?"

"Fred and Duke went to school together. After Fred's divorce and losing you, he became part of our family. I don't remember a holiday get-together when he wasn't there. Or funeral. After—after the accident, you could say he and Uncle Duke finished raising me. Fred taught me everything I know about horses and cattle, and the chief added most of what they didn't teach me in the police academy."

"Did Fred like anyone besides you and your uncle?" Mack asked the question for an excuse to continue studying her profile and admire the perfection of her skin in the surreal light. The answer was almost irrelevant.

"Of course. But he didn't trust easily. That's probably something you two would have found you had in common." As they passed the entryway of a ranch with an electronic gate and pole fencing freshly painted green, she nodded. "That's us. Pretty Pines."

The visuals failed to trigger even the slightest memory in Mack. "Did we ever meet? I have to admit I remember less than I thought I did."

"I'm guessing you and your mother left about the time that I was born. I may have been all of six when you last visited as a teenager. That would have made me invisible to you. And the pole fence wouldn't have been there yet. We still used barbed and ranch wire back then. Here we are," she added, turning into the next driveway.

As she parked before the simple gate with the metal letters *Last Call Ranch* bolted to it, Mack remembered his father's irreverent humor in naming the place and his mother's chastising him for making them the town trash. Her protests had seemed hypocritical even to a kid of eight who'd witnessed how much both of his parents drank—and the fights that followed. Now they struck him as doubly so, considering the line of work she'd ended up in.

"You have the keys."

Pulled back to the present, Mack dug out two sets from the envelope. There were about a dozen keys on each ring. Alana pointed to the correct set and, once he handed it to her, deftly flipped to the sturdy stainless key.

"All of the house keys and the front-gate key are on this one. You'll soon memorize them because I color coded them. The other ring is for the barn, truck and equipment."

Accepting the handful, Mack went to open the gate, attempting to move as normally as possible. He would definitely look into getting an electronic gate system like the Anderses had, and not just because of the convenience. He had to shift to use the patrol car's headlights to get the lock released, which would be more of a pain in bad weather than it already was. Besides, the fancier gizmo might help sell the place faster—not that he was planning to do that.

Oh, yes, you are.

Back in the car, he saw a front-door light and a security light by the barn. When they came to the ranch house, he saw it would take more than a fancy front gate to entice a buyer. The house was white brick with plain windows adorned with cheap miniblinds and a white metal roof. There were no shrubs around the place, and maybe the pastures were well tended, but the yard looked like it was nothing but weeds. He'd seen military barracks that looked more inviting.

"Home sweet home," he muttered with a sinking feeling.

"It could be. It just needs a little TLC. Eberardo has had his hands full with the animals." Alana put the vehicle in Park. "Do you want me to show you where the important things are?"

"I shouldn't take up any more of your time."

As he began to reach for the door handle again, Alana touched his arm. "Wait."

Mack turned back in surprise. When he saw her pensive look, curiosity got the best of him.

"You need to know something, and I'd like you to

hear it from me rather than just reading it cold and mis-understanding. In the will," she said, nodding to the envelope in his grasp, "Fred was concerned that something might have happened to you before he actually passed—or that somehow the place would end up on the auction block, or worse."

Mack raised an eyebrow. "What would he have considered worse?"

"Your mother sweeping in and taking possession."

Mack grunted. That would have done it, he thought wryly. "So what did he do? Just spit it out," he ordered, as she continued to hesitate.

"He adjusted his will so that if you died, or if you relinquish claim on the estate, it falls to me."

Chapter Two

So that's what it took to break the iron man's enigmatic stare and impressive control, Alana thought, as the news registered in Mack's expression. But she couldn't blame him for being slow to reply. She'd been bowled over herself when Fred announced his decision some six months ago.

"Congratulations," Mack finally said.

His tone left little to imagine about his mindset. "Don't make it sound like that. I tried to talk him out of it."

"I'm sure you did."

"Yes. I did."

"But the fact that you didn't convince him tells me that he hoped in the end that you would get the place. He really didn't want me to have it."

"That's not true. He was sorry about your broken relationship, but so much time had passed, he didn't know where to begin trying to mend things."

"I could have my own family, who might need a decent home, or help that this could provide," Mack said, nodding in the direction of the house.

"Do you?"

"No."

She'd gathered as much already, by the way he was traveling and from what he'd said earlier, but she couldn't help but feel an odd relief at hearing him confirm it. "Well, I'm sorry if his decision offends, but the fact remains that he was determined to keep your mother off the ranch." What he'd actually said was that he would "volunteer for hell first," and had insisted to Alana that she was more family to him than his own flesh and blood was.

"That much I understand," Mack said in reference to his mother. "I remember some whopper yelling matches between those two."

"Uncle Duke pretty much said the same thing." Alana slid him a sidelong look. "Do you know where she is these days?"

"The last contact I had with her, she was wanting to borrow an additional twenty thousand to add to the percentage she owned in a strip joint she managed in California."

"You're serious?"

"That was pretty much my reaction to her. Needless to say, she hasn't been in touch since."

That was some story *not* to pass on to his children—if he ever had any. "So you're okay now?"

"With her choices?" Mack's lips twisted with distaste. "Who can ever be okay with that? But it's her business."

"I meant with my news."

"Well, it could be worse," he drawled. "If my father was anything like my mother, I could be stuck with having to call you 'Mom.'"

Alana pursed her lips, thinking he didn't realize how close he came to the truth. "At one point, that was his plan."

Mack's eyes narrowed. "That son of a—"

"Calm down. I pretended that he was joking." He didn't need to know that she'd left in complete emotional turmoil and had immediately saddled her horse and had ridden for hours to deal with her feelings. "At any rate, it didn't happen."

"Probably not for lack of trying." Mack's gaze swept over her. "Were you ever lovers?"

Alana matched him stare for stare. "I told you that he and Uncle Duke finished raising me. What do you think?"

"I think that it sounded like a win-win situation for you."

To some, Alana thought. The most mercenary. But Fred's thinking had been all pragmatism just as his instincts were that of a caretaker, even then. He'd reasoned that, since she didn't seem in any hurry to let any "young rooster" sweep her off her feet, they could marry and merge Last Call and Pretty Pines. That would give them twice the clout in the community and keep it out of the hands of developers and a certain bottled-water company that wanted the aquifer water the ranch sat on. Alana also knew Fred's other motivation—that he had shared Uncle Duke's worry that the loss of her brother and parents had changed her forever, that maybe with more responsibility or his—what? Attention? Influence? That she would quit risking her neck on over-spirited horses and handling the night shift that no one else wanted for exactly those reasons.

"I loved Fred," she reiterated. "But I wasn't about to expose either of us to the gossip and taunts that were likely to follow from agreeing to marry him. And I never could have taken him as a lover." She gestured again to the keys he held. "But all that is immaterial now. You're here and I'm out of the picture."

"Are you? Let's see," Mack replied.

Too late, Alana realized what he was up to. Before she could stop him, he reached over to cup the back of her head, and pressed his lips to hers.

At first, she just tried to push him away. It wasn't her intent to injure—she understood the rush of emotions that he was experiencing. She could feel his anger at Fred, even his hurt, and she was the closest thing to being able to strike out at him. But she also had to make Mack realize how wrong and off base he was in pulling this stunt. Then, before she could do more than grip his wrists, he softened the kiss.

The change had her momentarily hesitating, and that was a mistake. It lowered her guard enough for her to realize how wonderful his lips felt against hers, caressing and coaxing, even yearning. She hadn't been kissed in a while—her choice—and never with this kind of wistful persuasion. It undermined her ability to keep her heart steeled against feelings, and crept under her defenses to remind her that she was all too human, and the world was fast becoming a lonelier place.

Just when she began to reach for his face to trace the sharp contours, she found herself released. When she opened her eyes, Mack was opening the door.

"That's what I thought," he muttered, before slamming the door shut behind him.

That had been a damned foolish thing to do, Mack thought as Alana spun the patrol car into a sharp U-turn the second he had his duffel bag, and sped down the driveway. She also pulled out into the street and burned rubber as she drove away, leaving the front gate open. It could have been worse. She could have taken off with his bag. Bottom line, he didn't regret it. Another couple hundred feet of walking in pain to lock up would be a small price to pay for getting under Alana Anders's skin the way she had his.

He'd wanted to kiss her at first sight. Okay, soon after he first looked over and realized the smoky-voiced female asking about his welfare wasn't a figment of his imagination. So things hadn't gone as he would have liked thereafter, but then he always expected to be let down by people. It was a lesson learned in the volatile company of his parents. In this case, the price had been worth it. He'd wanted to find out what Alana's game was. But soon his focus had been sheer lust and, in hindsight, he wasn't one bit sorry—even if she came back in an hour with a warrant for assault of an officer.

After returning from locking the gate, he used the front-door light to locate the correct key to the house. Once inside, he flipped on inside switches and set his duffel bag against an old buffet. He was in a breakfast nook that opened to the kitchen.

"Yeah," he murmured, remembering. "But somebody washed the cherry pie and beer off the walls."

It was also warmer than he preferred. Not summer in Iraq or Afghanistan warm, but the outdoors at this hour was almost more pleasant. No doubt Alana kept the air conditioner set higher to save on utility bills. He went in search of the thermostat, found it and dropped the gauge ten degrees.

Cripes, the place looked dated, he thought. Mack actually started to remember the layout of the furniture— the mud-brown recliner in front of the TV—although it was a flat-screen now, not the monster casing that looked like it would need the "jaws of life" to crack it open. However, the striped red-and-blue couch, the wrought-iron-and-glass coffee table, the gaudy lamps that looked like they'd been picked up at somebody's idea of a flea market, were all unpleasantly familiar. Oddly enough, he doubted his mother couldn't do worse even after all these years. At least there weren't any bead curtains in doorways. He did, however, catch a lingering hint of cigar smoke.

A bonfire seemed to be in order. No doubt Alana would suggest a garage sale or donation to some charity. The thought came as soon as he caught sight of a photo of her on the side table beside the recliner...and another by one of the lamps.

"Whatever happens first," he muttered to himself. "It'll sell faster empty."

Having ventured this far, he wandered from the living room down a hall, to an office-den where he noticed there were numerous photographs on display. Once again most were of Alana, or included her. Alana with both his father and what he suspected was her uncle. Alana and her horse, her dog, her first car… everything but brushing her teeth, Mack thought with mild sarcasm. There was no denying she was a heartbreaker—had been even as a baby—but by the time she was a teenager, she'd looked like a ghost of herself. He suspected they must have been taken soon after her brother and parents died. The more recent ones—photos of being awarded ribbons and trophies at rodeo and equestrian events—showed a perfected smile. Mack narrowed his eyes as he studied them more closely. No, he wasn't wrong. None of the smiles quite reached her haunted brown eyes. Nevertheless, Mack thought as he felt a twist in his belly and tightening in his loins, she was something.

"Damn it," he muttered, setting down the last photo.

A quick check of the rest of the house had him deciding to put his duffel bag in the second bedroom that he thought he remembered was his. At least he remembered the queen-size bed when he'd last been here. The thing was barely large enough to handle his growing body then. It wouldn't provide a great sleep tonight, but he couldn't think of sleeping in his father's bed. Not tonight after what Alana had confessed. Maybe never.

All he wanted was a shower, a drink and a few

hours' escape from any more thinking, even though that's what he'd also come here to do. But the future suddenly seemed as unpleasant as the past.

"You better not have drunk all the bourbon, you old buzzard," he muttered, stripping off his T-shirt.

"On to the next chapter," Alana murmured, as she turned her silver pickup into Pretty Pines Ranch the next morning. Not even her late aunt's sweet coining of the property's name could bring a smile to her lips as it usually did. She was running late and knew that Duke would be making breakfast, with one ear tuned to the police-scanner radio, an eye on the TV on the kitchen counter catching up on the morning news, and everything else directed at the driveway, waiting for her arrival. Nothing had changed since the accident—she could barely think the word *crash,* let alone say it—and that was mostly her fault. She'd given her uncle no reason to stop worrying about her. From the time she arrived for work at the station every afternoon, until she returned home in the morning—in fact, any minute that she wasn't asleep in her own bed—he stressed. Countless sessions with doctors, psychiatrists…even lectures and threats from Duke hadn't achieved much. She still lived with her torment and pain. But she did her best to make sure he knew that she *did* adore him.

The widower cop had been the center of her universe—more like her anchor—since their world turned inside out. That was saying something considering that he looked like your stereotypical drill instructor and had a personality to match, particularly when someone crossed him, or one of his officers caused him trouble or embarrassment. But even when she was the one on the receiving end of his wrath, Alana loved no one more; however, she still hoped that with Mack's arrival, Duke would now take a little of that intensive watchfulness off her.

"Morning, handsome," she called with determined brightness, upon entering the sun-filled white-on-white kitchen. Immediately, unfastening her paraphernalia-heavy belt, she beamed at him as she set it on the breakfast-table chair to the left of the one she would be using. Duke stood by the stove dressed in his summer blues with one of her aunt Sarah's aprons over it. She could already smell his *Brut* cologne before she reached him to rise on tiptoe and kiss him just beside his ear. "You smell better than the bacon."

Duke Anders pretended to swat at her as she stole a piece. "Don't play me, young lady. You're late. Imagine what I thought when I called the station to see what was keeping you, since there was nothing of importance happening on the radio. Then to learn that Eisley had taken his patrol car—on time and properly clean, lucky for you—and that you weren't at your desk completing reports."

Alana made a face at the mention of her day-shift counterpart and ripped a piece of bacon off the strip to pop it into her mouth. "Phil was born with the wrong chromosomes. He's as finicky as some prissy Southern belle. Plus he won't ever stop believing day-shift personnel have seniority over us night crawlers. Is he still whining about the bag with the bottle of water and empty bag of chips that I accidentally left in the car the other day?"

"Procedure is set for a purpose," Duke recited in a tone that exposed he'd done it numerous times. "You leave the vehicle as clean and full of fuel as you found it."

"It was water and a wrapper, not a box of tampons."

He grimaced as though she'd uttered a vulgarity. "Do you mind? I'm cooking here."

Alana popped the rest of the bacon into her mouth on her way to the coffeemaker where her red mug was set, waiting for her. She wasn't about to tell him that she'd stopped at the grocery store and picked up a few things that she planned to carry next door as soon as he left for the station.

"I went to the cemetery."

"Oh."

It wasn't a fib—she had gone, only not after her shift change. She'd done so under cover of darkness, which she often did because she didn't like or need people spying on her and the gossips saying, "Did you hear? Ally was back at the cemetery. As much time as she spends there, you'd think she can't wait to join her family." She *had* touched her mom's and dad's and Chase's gravestones, which were in the same row, but she'd gone to tell Fred what she hoped he already knew—that his son had returned.

"Are you okay?"

Filling her mug halfway from the machine that was the same as the one she'd put at the station, Alana returned to watch Duke work. "Sure. But I guess this is where you tell me that you already know something you think I'd hide from you?"

He flipped their hash browns a last time and then cracked one egg for her sunny-side-up preference and two for his over-easy choice. "Yeah, I'll admit I thought you were going to try to sneak the news about the Graves boy by me. I should have known you felt Fred should hear the news first."

And he did, Alana thought, smiling into her mug. "Mack is hardly a boy anymore. He's thirty-eight and barely shorter than you, but he looks like he could bench press your weight with no problem." At her uncle's scowl, she added, "No, Bunny didn't exaggerate this time. What she doesn't know is that he's retired from the marine corps and came by on his way to nowhere to see if he could make peace with his father."

"That was decent of him." Duke sounded approving, despite his downturned mouth. "How did he take the news?"

"Exactly as you would expect of a soldier." In her mind, Alana relived the scene. "Don't forget, they were strangers and hadn't parted on the best terms. But I felt he was truly sorry."

"Not so sorry that he wanted to try again over the twenty years."

"Well, maybe Fred took the answer to that to his grave with him, but that communication thing works both ways. Besides, he's done tours in both Iraq and Afghanistan, and who knows where else before that. Cut him some slack."

Duke nodded as he digested that. "God bless him,

then. And I wasn't being judgmental, I was just curious."

Alana leaned her head against his shoulder and rubbed his broad back. "I know."

"I take it that you brought him next door?"

"It was foolish for him to insist he could walk when he was obviously sore. It seems he's been hitching and hiking his way here all the way from the East Coast. So, after having him sign the appropriate paperwork, I called Eberardo to give him a heads-up, and drove Mack, yes."

As her uncle put her egg on her platter, along with a portion of the hash browns and bacon, he handed it over, asking, "So? What do you think of him? He sounds like a fine specimen of manhood. If he didn't inherit Fred's ugly mug."

"OMG," Alana groaned. "You're worse than Bunny. When I called in that I was checking out someone along the creek, she went into some nonsense about blue moons."

Duke frowned as he plated his breakfast. "Was there a toxic spill in the area that I missed on the radio?"

"My thought exactly." Leading the way to the table, she saw a way to get him away from his rabid matchmaking focus. "I told him about the will." She'd never disclosed anything about Fred's proposal to her uncle, afraid that it would upset Duke and forever alter the two friends' relationship—if not destroy it. But she had shared the rest.

Sighing as he relieved his legs of some weight, Duke opined, "Bet he loved that."

"You can say that again." Remembering that kiss forced Alana to take her time with her napkin and taking a slice of toast from the plate on the center of the table. Her lips all but tingled as though she was reliving the experience again. "Why do you always make the toast first? It's practically as hard as Sheetrock."

"Don't exaggerate. You can inhale your weight in those stale croutons they put on your Caesar salad at Doc's, but you're faulting my toast?"

"Now you sound like an indignant wife, all puffed up," she teased.

"And you sound like an ungrateful husband," Duke muttered. "Get back on topic."

Instead, Alana took a big bite of toast with jam and chewed. The later it grew, the more compelled her uncle would be to get to the station. He was determined to retire with the pride of knowing that he'd probably had the best attendance record of most police chiefs in Texas, and a more impressive tardiness record.

"Ally, how did he take the news about the will?"

"He now thinks I'm a Jezebel. The kids today would just say 'ho,' but it all amounts to the same thing. He's concluded I used my feminine charms to con Fred into making me the alternate heir."

Duke's eyes bulged. He stopped in midchew.

"Swallow, please," Alana directed. "It's a completely rational reaction if you consider what his opinion of women must be after what he learned about them through experiencing his mother's behavior."

"I can worry about you," Duke said, poking his chest

with his thumb. "People can gossip because you drive like you're auditioning for a NASCAR sponsorship—"

"I was very respectful of the speed limit driving Mack to Last Call."

"—but nobody calls you...that!"

As Duke's fist struck the table, the reverberations had Alana lifting her mug to keep coffee from splashing into her plate. "One bright spot." Alana continued to soothe him. "Fred can rest in peace knowing Mack doesn't seem to have a cozy relationship with Dina."

Duke's coloring slowly eased to a mild pink. "Is that so?"

"He didn't sound like he would be heading there anytime soon, even if things hadn't worked out for him here."

"You covered a lot of ground."

"It's a long shift."

Looking as though he had a few choice things to remind her about that, Duke managed to settle down and instead ask, "Where is she these days?"

"Managing a strip club in California."

Her uncle slumped back in his chair and looked toward the ceiling. "You called it, Fred." To Alana, he explained, "He said she would squander the money he gave her in the divorce settlement, and take the boy to ruination, too."

"Uncle Duke, you're sounding a bit like an offended mother-in-law. From the rest of what I learned so far, Mack didn't have much of a childhood once they left here, but he's made a life for himself that he can be proud of."

"Let's hope you're right about that." Duke returned to his meal and took another bite. "Did you tell me if he's married? I forget."

The wily fox never forgot anything, but Alana let that slide. "Not married. No children."

"At thirty-eight?"

Of course, people of her uncle's generation would think there was something wrong with that. "If he's gay, my antenna is way, way off," Alana replied, again thinking of the kiss. "But I meant what I said—don't even think of matchmaking."

"Fine. Send me to my grave without a great-niece or -nephew to spoil."

"If that's the way it works out, you have my apologies. *You* can apologize for throwing every male at me that passes through the city limits."

"I do skip bona fide transients and felons. One of us has to pay attention to your biological clock."

Alana's mirthless laugh had an edge. There was no denying he did that. "Hasn't it crossed your mind that he could be a post-traumatic-stress candidate, a walking powder keg waiting to go off? Leave him alone and give him a chance to come to terms with this loss. He's already a tired soldier."

With that, she attacked her food in all seriousness and ate in record speed. Inevitably, her uncle noticed.

"In a hurry to meet the sandman?" he drawled. "You never do sleep well, and never at all on a full stomach."

"Don't plan to sleep. I plan to change and get to the barn and work on Tanker. If the abscess in that tooth is completely gone, he needs to start being worked again."

"Does that include a ride to Last Call? I've yet to meet the man who can resist the picture you make when you're on a horse. Not that you seem to notice."

"If I head that way, it'll be because I jumped every other fence and tree and creek on this place," she said, although she knew what that would do to him.

Duke turned pale. "Try to remember people count on you to show up for your shift this afternoon."

"I never forget," she said softly. That was the problem.

After Duke left and once Alana changed into jeans along with one of Chase's big football jerseys from UT—just in case Mack Graves got the wrong idea and thought she was intent on seducing him—she locked up the house and headed for her truck. She did intend to check Tanker, but first she wanted to deliver a plate of breakfast to go with the supplies she'd bought for next door. She'd done much the same thing for months when Fred got increasingly weaker. It was what neighbors should do, she assured herself, and Mack was Fred's son, so it was, in a way, like helping Fred. But no matter how hard she tried to justify her actions, she knew she was at least partly kidding herself.

The man had triggered something inside her that was as powerful as an adrenaline rush. She'd often felt a similar thrill riding and sometimes driving, and occasionally when there was an arrest to be made on the job, but she'd never felt the same curiosity, let alone interest, in a man. That was saying something, when she'd been courted, and been the object of many a matchmaking scheme, and had even tried an affair or two. Mack's kiss made all of that pale in comparison. She wanted to discover if it had been a fluke. Of course it was, she assured herself quickly. But she doubted a fling with Mack was going to raise her uncle's blood pressure the way some of her other behavior did.

As she closed the gate between their properties, she spotted Eberardo emerging from the barn, Two Dog, the cow-dog-mix canine, only steps behind him. Eberardo waved and met her at the house.

A few inches shorter than her and perhaps five years older, he was a nice-looking man with a quick smile and a gentle hand with livestock. Fred had hired him over a dozen years ago on a temporary basis, but soon moved the trailer in to make the job permanent.

"Buenos días!" she said, as she emerged from the truck with the covered plate and the two bags of groceries. The dog jumped high to sniff at the plate. "Nothing for you this trip," she told him. "I promise, next time."

Eberardo sharply ordered Two Dog to sit and the dog immediately dropped to the ground, all obedience.

"I don't think Mr. Graves is up yet," Alana told Eberardo. "I was going to put this in his refrigerator."

The ranch hand tipped his straw Western hat in greeting. "Then I come back. I just wanted to check in case he don't want I stay." He wiped his hands with a red kerchief that he pushed back into his jeans pocket. "I don't want no trouble."

Alana hadn't seen him so nervous since he'd come to Last Call looking for work. "Eberardo, this is your home, and Mr. Mack doesn't know much about ranching. He'll need your knowledge and advice."

"*Gracias,* Señorita Ally. I hope you are right. I would like to stay."

Alana knew that was partly because he was in a relationship with a nurse at the local hospital. "Then we'll work toward that goal. Mack Graves seems a decent man."

That's what Mack heard as he opened the side door. At the sound of the approaching vehicle—and knowing he'd locked the gate last night—he'd managed to drag on jeans and had hoped to pull on the T-shirt he'd grabbed, but he had to settle for holding it between his hands. Most of what he wanted to cover was on his back, anyway.

"I'll take that as a compliment," he said, allowing himself a swift head-to-toe review of the woman who'd even intruded into his dreams. His first thought was that if she had put on that big jersey hoping to make herself less appealing, she'd failed. His second was an unexpected twist of jealousy as he wondered who it had belonged to.

Although Alana merely lifted her left eyebrow at his perusal, she turned to the man beside her. "Mack, this is Eberardo Chavez, whom I told you about. Eberardo, this is Mack Graves, Mr. Fred's son. Anything you need or don't understand," she added to Mack, "he's your walking resource center. He's also a darned good mechanic, and helped teach me a lot of what I know about horses."

Eberardo grinned, his white teeth brilliant in his

bronzed face and his eyes twinkling with pride. "Nobody as good with the critters like you, Señorita Ally."

While Mack knew he still looked bleary-eyed despite having showered, he shook Eberardo's hand firmly. "Good to meet you. Would you and *Ally* like to come in for some—I was about to look if there was any coffee in the pantry."

"Is okay, *señor.* I must get back to work. Please, if you need Eberardo, you yell or honk the truck or tractor horns, or Señorita Ally give you my cell phone number." He pulled it out of his pocket to confirm that it was charged and ready. "I come quick from any place."

"That sounds like a deal." Mack watched as the man and the white-and-black canine took off before returning his gaze to Alana. He caught that while he'd been focusing on Fred's hand, she was paying him back for his inspection. "Like what you see?"

"You live up to marine standards."

"Shouldn't you be getting your beauty sleep?"

"If I get three or four hours, I'm good." She nodded at her bounty. "I stopped at the market on the way home to pick up some essentials to buy you a little time before you make your presence known in town. Plus Uncle Duke tends to cook enough for four. Are you going to invite me in or was last night a hint that I should be intimidated by you?"

"I believe hints are a waste of time with you." But Mack allowed the smile tugging at his lips and stepped back to let her pass.

Alana carried everything to the kitchen table and, once he shut the door, Mack used the chance to tug on the white T-shirt, but he tried to move too fast and messed up the bandages on his back. He tried to untangle the tape from the shirt, and swore softly at the sting that told him that he failed. That's when he heard a gasp.

"Mack!"

So much for trying to keep the wounds private. He knew she was seeing the effects of the two bullets he'd taken during his final deployment. He had returned to wearing the bandages because of the chafing caused by his clothing, as well as the occasional bump of the duffel bag during countless miles of hiking.

"That'll teach me to finish dressing before answering the door," he said as she came to offer assistance. "I can get this."

"Oh, yeah, you're doing such an outstanding job. Hold still."

In short order, she removed the mangled mess and dabbed the antibiotic ointment from his T-shirt with the clean side of the gauze. "Take off this thing before you really start bleeding again." Without waiting for him to comply, she started tugging it over his head.

Mack helped finish, but gave her a warning look. "I'm fine."

"Of course you are," she replied, her tone mocking. "Sit. I'll start a pot of coffee and get you patched up. I take it there's more of that stuff in the bathroom?"

"Yeah."

Alana went to the refrigerator and took out a can of coffee. "Store the stuff in there," she said as though confident he was watching her. "It stays fresh longer."

"Far too complicated. That's why I've stuck with

instant for years," Mack said—but he was glad to take a seat and watch her. She was all efficiency and grace, no wasted movements.

"This is the same unit that's at the station," she said, filling the carafe from the refrigerator water dispenser. Then she counted three of the measuring scoops of grains into the filter. "Don't even attempt to tell me— this is a waste of your precious time."

Mack had to pinch the bridge of his nose to keep from laughing. The woman was as much a pain in his backside as she was irresistible.

Once she turned on the machine, she vanished around the corner and down the hall in search of the first-aid supplies. Mack used the break to peel apart the aluminum foil around the platter to get a slice of the bacon. Its scent was making him salivate.

"That needs to go into the microwave," Alana said upon her return. "It'll taste better warm."

"Tastes fine to me," he said, knowing his stubbornness would irk.

Instead of replying, she simply plucked the plate out of his reach, tore off the rest of the foil and placed his meal in the microwave. In about half a minute, she took it out, pulled a fork from the silverware drawer and set everything in front of him.

"My, you *do* know your way around here," Mack drawled.

"I told you, this was my second home, and when Fred wouldn't let the nurses come any longer, I took care of him." With Mack focused on the food, Alana set to work on his back. "Dear God, how did those bullets miss vital organs? It looks as though you were almost killed."

"Almost doesn't count."

She used peroxide to clean the areas again. "The wounds don't look very old."

"July Fourth."

"Should you even be out of the hospital yet? Your cross-country trek doesn't seem to have been the wisest idea."

"Tell the chief that he makes a mean breakfast."

Taking the strong hint, Alana stopped asking questions. Mack could tell she had performed first aid before and had a gentle touch. No doubt she'd made his father's last days more bearable; he certainly enjoyed her ministrations. He let himself imagine her fingers moving elsewhere, until his body told him that he was asking for trouble.

"I didn't mean that you had to go mute on me."

"You grouse just like Uncle Duke. Your wish is my command, master," she added, bending to coo near his ear.

Mack decided she could probably do good-cop-bad-cop all by her lonesome and make it sexy. "Everything all right at the station?"

"Yep," she replied, once again the girl next door. "You were the highlight of our shift. Well, Ed thought he could catch a suspicious vehicle probably transporting drugs through town, but he had to pass the call to the state police once they left our jurisdiction."

That tidbit of information had Mack's fantasy of kissing her again go up in smoke. "Do you get a lot of that?"

"Worried for me, gyrene? Or are you just trying to keep me from asking why your seven-week-old wounds are reopening?"

"Why don't you sit on my lap and we'll discuss it?"

"I may be tempted, but I'm not easy." Finished with her task, she threw the mangled bandages into the trash canister near the back door. Then she went to wash her hands at the sink. When she was done, she poured Mack a mug of coffee and brought it to the table, then sat down beside him. "I'm going to do something I rarely do and that's ask a favor. Please let Eberardo know soon that he can stay on."

Mack planned to anyway, not just because things looked well tended, but because he suspected he wouldn't be here to see to things himself. But Alana's request brought out the devil's advocate in him. "Because?"

"These are challenging times. He was born in the U.S., but not everyone treats him as though he was—especially now that Fred is gone. They wouldn't dare do it before. Add to that, he hasn't been lucky in love. His fiancée left him for his best friend. He's finally in a relationship with a nurse at the hospital, who seems to have her head straight on her shoulders. It would be great if he could stay close to her in order to see if things work out between them."

"I'll bow to your experienced judgment, how's that? After all, you are the heir-in-waiting."

Alana cast him a droll look, then carried his empty plate to the sink. When she returned with the coffee-pot, Mack lifted his mug for a refill.

"What does your uncle say about you coming over here?"

"He thinks I'm working on Tanker."

"I thought in the pictures I've seen that he turned gray prematurely," Mack mused.

With a sigh, Alana admitted, "Yeah, that and the perpetual frown between his eyebrows is mostly me."

"Knowing that, I'd think you'd have pity on the poor guy."

"I would if I could shut off my mind." She shrugged. "Doctors wrote prescriptions, but their ideas about solutions just turned me into a zombie."

Mack would have liked to hear more, but she rose, signaling that she was ready to leave. "If Tanker is a dog," he said to delay her, "your grocery bill must be something else."

"It's worse than that, he's my horse. Seventeen hands of black Westphalian beauty." At Mack's confused expression, she explained, "That's how horses are measured. You take its height from hooves to withers and divide those inches by four, which is the size of a palm. In other words, he's five-six. He eats like a pregnant sow, too, but he's family. Fortunately for him—and us—our second business is cattle. So I help out Eberardo when he needs a hand with your stock and he helps with ours. I hope you won't mind it staying that way. Well, at least until you get competent with the cattle yourself."

"I may not be around long enough to achieve that." He nodded to the groceries. "What do I owe you for those?"

"Your presence," she replied. "Stay, Mack. Last Call is your birthright. Fred spent his life turning it into what it is and ached for you to do more than accept it. He hoped that someday you would embrace it."

She sounded so earnest. Hell, Mack thought, she looked close to crying. He had to do something before he took her into his arms and made promises he shouldn't. "I told you, I don't know anything about ranching. And the truth is, I'm not sure that I want to learn. All I know is soldiering."

She went ramrod straight, but she didn't back down. "Let me guess...you have an offer by some civilian security firm that'll take you back overseas as soon as you heal? Or is strip-club mama thinking you'd make a good bouncer while you learn her business?"

As passion simmered and their gazes remained locked, Mack said slowly, "That...I would never do."

"I suppose that's one thing we can be grateful for."

"Instead of jumping to conclusions about other people, you might try straightening out your own life."

The flash of pain in the depths of her eyes was almost palpable. Mack was sorry to learn his ability to hurt with words remained as keen as his marksmanship, but he'd met his match in guts and willpower in this woman, and this was no time to back down.

"I've done my share," she said at last. "I promised Uncle Duke that I wouldn't get on a plane again."

"As long as he's alive?" Mack was sensing a daredevil with a subconscious death wish, although he wished he didn't. "So instead you drive around at night flirting with the idea that some loser high on meth, or heaven knows what, will show up and put you out of your misery?"

Drawing a labored breath, Alana stepped around him. "This has been a blast, but I've had my fill of psychoanalysis. You win, gyrene. You live your life and I'll live mine."

Mack took hold of her wrist. It wasn't a threatening move—he knew his strength—in fact he was intentionally gentle and stroked his thumb against her soft skin to reassure her. "Ally...wait. I'm sorry."

"Let me go."

"I had no right to say that, particularly when I live with my own demons," he confessed. "The truth is that I don't think I can stay because...I can't risk being found."

Chapter Three

Whatever Alana was expecting, it wasn't that admission. "What are you talking about?" she demanded, extricating herself from his grasp. "I ran your license through the computer after I dropped you off here, and not only are there no warrants out on you, you don't even have a ticket to blush over."

"Maybe not being in-country much had a little to do with that," Mack drawled.

Feasible, but Alana's mind was racing ninety miles an hour as she waited on him to be more forthcoming. No doubt her uncle had done his own checking upon reaching the station, and if he had come up with anything, her cell phone would be going crazy by now, and the secured front gate would be forced.

Mack sighed. "Relax, it's nothing like what you're obviously thinking—although I'm sure certain people wouldn't mind putting me in the brig, or insist on another mental evaluation on top of those that are mandatory at the end of every deployment."

"Oh, yeah, that was reassuring."

"I'm trying." Mack started to reach for her again, caught himself and, running his hand over his hair, turned away. "You're right about the fact that I should still be in the hospital—or should have stayed longer than I did. But when I learned that they wanted to give me a citation, I didn't hang around to accept it."

She just knew those wounds had been a result of something very brave and heroic. "You risked your health for *that?* What kind of citation?" she asked, her suspicion growing.

"It's the Navy Cross."

Thinking of a young soldier who was recently in the news for resisting the Medal of Honor, she didn't bother asking why on earth Mack was refusing his award. If he was anywhere close to being as modest, she had to respect his choice as much as she admired his valor. "That's a big deal."

"It should be."

"But you don't believe you deserve it?"

"I know I don't."

There was only one question to ask. "Will you tell me what happened?"

"No."

She expected that blunt reply. She was private in her own way, but he was a black hole in comparison. On the other hand, how did you escape the United States Government? "Isn't it the Secretary of the Navy who presents those? You left the hospital knowing that you were snubbing him?"

"I didn't snub anyone, I politely but firmly said at the moment they gave me the news that I don't believe I deserve it." He did, however, give her a wary glance. "So no one has gone into my records enough to realize I have a father here and tried to contact him?"

"Is your answering machine full of calls? I know there's been nothing happening at the police station. But wait a minute—isn't this akin to being AWOL or something?"

"I did enough paperwork in the hospital that they can't legitimately call me that. I can imagine a few people are ticked off, though. You don't deny the brass their chances in front of cameras."

Alana had to agree there. They had experienced enough situations in their little town to confirm that you didn't deny politicians their publicity, either. But thinking about how weak he must have been to start a journey from Virginia to Texas on foot, how risky that had been, she shook her head. "Are you sure that you don't want to contact your mother to let her know you're alive? What if they've contacted her?"

"Then I hope she has the decency to tell them that we haven't been in touch in years and otherwise stays away from TV cameras."

That was a hard perspective, but Alana hadn't experienced what he obviously had at her hands. "I'm sorry that you grew up in a broken home. Sorry that you were taken away from this." She gestured toward the window and the hundreds of acres of pristine pasture, ponds. "Maybe it wouldn't have taught you the survival instincts your street education obviously did, but you definitely wouldn't be in a hurry to walk away as you are now."

"Street education," Mack said with a snort. "Talk about understatements. My mother never wanted me, she took me to win against the old man, that's all. Once she hooked up with Vince, the creep who convinced her to invest her divorce settlement into his business, I was an inconvenience. But she still wouldn't let me come back here. You know what kind of schools you attend when you live in neighborhoods where those clubs are located?"

"I don't want to imagine," Alana replied. "It's a testament to your strength that you got through it."

"Got through alive."

Accepting that there was nothing she could say that would soften the scorn Mack felt for the years he'd struggled to survive, and the people who put him through that, Alana sought to focus on what she *could* do. "You're clearly looking to start over yet again. Or at least do some serious thinking. I'll say it again—this is the place for you. I just feel it." At his first sign of frustration, she reached out to touch his arm in an appeal to hear her out. "You can still keep a low profile for a while. Eberardo will understand and assist you. I can talk to him if you prefer, and I'll help, too."

"Don't even think of turning me into your pet patient," Mack all but growled. "I'm not my father, and I sure as hell don't need you."

He didn't just stiff-arm people, he pushed them away.

It was ironic that having lost most of her family as she had, the gene that triggered fear had been pulverized by that experience.

"Your father wasn't my pet anything," she said, all but going nose to nose with him. "He was a Texas cattleman—proud, ornery and determined. He may have hidden from you that his heart was broken, but at least he never once spoke to me the way you are."

"Then maybe talking is a waste."

This time when Mack kissed her, there wasn't the inconvenience of a patrol car's console and paraphernalia between them. This time he could sweep an arm around her waist and lock her against him so tightly there were few secrets left between them. Alana knew that he could feel she wore no bra beneath the jersey and tank top, and she could feel he was aroused even before he deepened the kiss into a sensual assault.

It was soon a toss-up as to whose heart pounded harder or faster. Alana knew she could end this easily enough. She had enough training in self-defense, although she knew his own skills—along with his size— would make any break of his hold only a temporary thing. Besides, his kisses were much better than his anger. Much.

When he lifted his head to suck in a much-needed breath, his challenge was as bold as his kisses had been. "You want me to stay? Make me."

Was he really challenging her to seduce him? In his condition? "I'm not going to be responsible for putting you back in the hospital."

"You think a lot of yourself," he taunted.

Alana refused to take the bait. "If you had an ounce of sense in that thick skull, you'd thank me. I've seen your back. There's no telling what you look like inside. Now it's still possible for you to live here quietly for another week or two. Recuperate from the damage you may have done to yourself. If you push your luck, as you are, when you do wind up hospitalized, the first thing they'll do is wire back east for your medical records, and all of your grand plans to hide from those looking for you will have been for nothing."

"Do I have your word that you'll see that others will keep my presence under wraps?"

Word could already be spreading around town. "I'll do what damage control I can, and I'm sure so will the chief as soon as I pass on your wishes. I don't know how successful he'll be if word has leaked to the editor-in-chief of the local newspaper."

"Are you trying to talk me into this idea of yours or out of it?" Mack demanded.

"I said I'll do everything I can. Do we have a deal?"

"Provided *you* also keep bringing me breakfast and keep my refrigerator stocked. Not Eberardo. You." After a pause, he added, "You can write yourself a check from the same checkbook you've been paying other bills with."

"You're lucky that I bank in the next town to avoid exactly the kind of gossip something like that would raise." Alana shook her head at what she was getting into. Duke definitely didn't need to know about these *finer* details. "I guess I can manage that for a week or so. But after that—"

"We renegotiate."

With an arch look, she asked, "Meaning by then you expect to feel well enough to include sex to the deal?"

"Oh, that's going to happen anyway."

While driving home, Alana called Eberardo's number and explained the way Mack wanted to work things for now. "I say this in confidence," she added to impart on him that his loyalty was critical. "Mack is still recovering from wounds. He needs another week or so before he should be moving around normally. The fewer people who know he's here recuperating, the easier it will be on him."

"Anything I can do, you let me know, Señorita Ally."

Alana knew to expect less enthusiasm and far more questions when she called her uncle. It would probably have been a good idea to drive into town, but her insides were still carrying the vibrations of Mack's kisses. If any of that showed in her eyes or behavior, Duke would see it.

"Can you talk?" she asked upon hearing his voice.

"Styles and Dodge are here, but we're done with business. Just shooting the breeze."

She could picture the burly man with a voice to match sitting with Mayor Jim Styles, a happily married father of four, and D.A. Lewis Dodge who, if it wasn't a court day, was probably dressed for fishing. "Did you say anything yet about our mutual new friend?"

"So far that sounds more like your description of the individual than mine, but to answer your question, no. It hasn't come up," Duke replied. "Hang on a second. Okay, gentlemen, I've got to get back to earning a nickel. See you at lunch, Jim."

Alana heard the murmur of farewells and then her uncle's grunt as he rose to shut his office door. "Sorry to intrude," she told him.

"To apologize you can tell me why you're on the phone at this hour and not sleeping." Duke replied. He grunted again as he resumed his seat.

Figuring her news would be explanation enough, she replied, "Mack has decided to hang around for a while. That decision comes with strings attached."

"Does it now? And how did you come by this information?"

Darn, she thought, he wasn't going to like this part. "I brought him breakfast. Look, he had nothing in the house and he wasn't even sounding agreeable to giving the place a chance. I learned there was an interesting reason for that attitude."

"I can't wait to hear it."

"He doesn't want his whereabouts known." The pause on her uncle's side of the phone spoke fathoms and Alana added quickly, "There's nothing on his record."

"Believe me, I'm aware of that. Do you think I didn't check myself first thing after I got here?"

The challenge would have had anyone in the office on pins and needles, but Alana thought she had the facts on her side. "His reason is entirely personal. He was wounded on his last deployment and he left the hospital before he should have. You see, he was supposed to receive the Navy Cross. Don't ask me for details, he refused to tell me. The point is that he doesn't want it."

"What kind of fool turns down that kind of honor?" Duke scoffed.

"A humble one? Someone who doesn't feel he deserves it?" Alana knew he remembered the recent incident in the news, too, because they'd discussed it.

"Well, son of a gun," her uncle muttered, as though speaking to himself.

"You haven't received any queries about him, have you?"

"If I had, do you think I'd be sitting here asking you what happened?" Duke's tone went from annoyed to concerned. "What is this about the hospital? How badly was he injured?"

"He was shot at least twice. I saw the wounds."

"And where on his anatomy are they located, or do I want to ask?"

"Don't be a prude, *Chief*."

"That's not your boss asking, it's your uncle, and you know it."

Unable to help it, Alana had to smile. "He was just tugging on a T-shirt when I arrived. Ask Eberardo. I also introduced them to each other. Mack messed up his bandages and, since they're on his back and hard to reach for him, I helped redo them."

"Are you sure he's not some deserter trying to cover up something?"

The resentful tone was as unkind as the suggestion. "That's a horrible thing to say!"

"I'm a cop, not a priest doling out absolution," Duke groused. "It's my job to weigh all possibilities."

"All he's asking is that we keep his arrival in town to ourselves as long as possible. He's dreading that the local newspaper will want to do a local-hero story—or, worse yet, the local TV stations."

"And how is he going to manage that and still eat? I guess there's always Eberardo to shop for him," Duke continued, as though thinking out loud. "Not that he's a town man, either. But he'll do it to keep his job."

Here goes nothing, Alana thought. "I'll do it. Eberardo has enough work on his hands."

That brought a stretch of silence from Duke. "I think I'll just take a ride over to Last Call and extend my own welcome," he finally said.

Alana knew it was useless to try to stop him, particularly once his mind was made up, but she hoped to at least delay him. "The front gate is locked."

"Oh, and I can't pick up the phone and tell him to unlock the thing?" her uncle challenged. "Or use the same gate you did?"

Accepting that she was beaten, she replied with equal feistiness, "Just don't honk or call me when you pass by. I'm heading for bed."

"It's about damned time!" Duke muttered, and hung up.

Mack wasn't thrilled to get the heads-up from Alana that her uncle was going to pay him a visit, but he appreciated that she'd stuck out her neck for him. As for the visit, he wasn't surprised. He knew without asking that she hadn't said anything about what had passed between them, and concluded the chief of police was curious as to what his old friend's son had amounted to, considering his full parentage. More likely the ex-marine wanted to determine for himself whether or not he was hiding something beyond the reason he'd given for wanting to keep a low profile.

However, and interestingly, the hour passed and Chief Duke Anders didn't show. Another hour went by, and then another. That's how Mack's day crawled by. It wasn't totally frustrating—he started to familiarize himself with the house. He began looking through old records to glean what it was he was being asked to take on, and finally made himself a sandwich from the supply of groceries Alana had brought over that morning. It still felt odd to be here, but his military life had taught him to adapt easily enough to location changes. Even his apartment back east didn't really feel like home, and despite the blandness of this decor, it wasn't a boiling or freezing tent in the environmental armpit of the world.

It was after four o'clock in the afternoon when, dozing on the couch, Mack heard a noise that sounded like a vehicle was approaching. He'd instantly checked his stainless waterproof wristwatch the moment he'd awakened and thought, *Alana should be clocking in about now.* Was the chief ready for his visit?

He came to the kitchen in time to see a police SUV pull up to the house. Although somewhat frustrated that he'd been kept in anticipation all day, Mack accepted he didn't know the older man's schedule and would give him the benefit of the doubt. On the other hand, the old codger probably knew that Alana would warn him, and pulled this on purpose.

He opened the door to the man he recognized mostly from photographs scattered around the house. Duke Anders now had wilder eyebrows, and a salt-and-pepper mix of color instead of the stark black shown in earlier photos. There was plenty of gray in his marine-burr haircut, as well. But his brown, eagle-sharp eyes remained clear. His waistline might be a few inches bigger, but Mack figured he was still capable of subduing a perp without too much trouble, if necessary.

"Heard you'd made it back." The lawman extended his hand as he approached Mack. "Welcome home."

Mack returned his powerful clasp. The trick was not to laugh out loud at the obvious power crunch. "Thank you…sir. Sorry that it's under these circumstances."

"That should be my line. This would have been a banner day for Fred."

While Mack gauged himself a couple of inches taller than Ally, Duke Anders stood another inch or two taller than him. After stepping back for him to enter, he shut the door, then gestured farther into the kitchen. "You should be off duty, and I was about to open a bottle of beer. Can I offer you one?"

"That sounds great. It's sure a miserable time of year to be in a dark uniform, even with the short sleeves. My predecessor never wore a uniform—it was always white cotton and jeans for him, and the Western hat. He liked to appear that he was still one of the fellows, but that seemed to compound some crime problems we had, so I made myself revert back." Duke accepted the bottle and saluted Mack with it. "Then again, where you've been, I imagine this heat is nothing."

Mack unscrewed his bottle's cap. "Once it gets over 105, it's all hell." He indicated the breakfast table. "Care to sit in here or would you prefer the living room?"

"This is perfect." In fact, Duke had already begun reaching for a chair before the words were out of Mack's mouth. "That room catches the afternoon sun. In summer, it's unbearable until almost bedtime."

"Yeah, I took a break from familiarizing myself with things and discovered that." The comment gave Mack the opportunity to tug at his damp T-shirt and pry it from his overheated skin. He'd turned down the air conditioner on his way to getting the door, but he didn't feel much relief yet. He took a swig of beer hoping none of the heat he was feeling was the return of a fever. The return of an infection was the last thing he needed. Hopefully what he was feeling was a simple case of nerves. After all, since he wouldn't be confronting his father, this was the next most important male to be facing around here.

Settling in the seat beside him, Mack watched Duke take a healthy swig of his drink. Except for those keen, dark eyes, he saw little of Ally in him. Of course, he preferred hers framed with lush lashes, especially when they twinkled with wicked humor and flashed with daring. There was something of a dare in Duke's gaze, too, though. Something like, *Think again if you plan to play fast and loose with my niece.*

"So what do you think?" he asked, as the older

man continued to study him. "I take it you're deciding whether or not I look anything like him?"

"There's enough Fred in you to assure your pedigree. Let's just hope your mother's contribution only went skin deep."

It was hard to keep from choking. The man was ten times as frank as Alana. "I'm starting to think surviving the marine corps was a breeze compared to this." Lifting his hands in surrender, he offered, "I'm not here to defend her or myself. I have my own feelings about my parentage. All I want is to mind my own business and not upset anyone else's."

After another studious stare, Duke asked, "And how does turning down that medal fit in that attitude? Seems to me you're upsetting someone's apple cart."

Mack nodded and started to attack the bottle's label with his thumbnail. "With all due respect, sir, that's my business. Suffice it to say, I didn't do anything except my job. Even at that, I wasn't successful."

"Are you the only one to get out alive?"

Mack just met his direct gaze, but refused to say more.

Grunting, Duke continued, "That's all I need around here, another person who doesn't sleep worth a damn. Are you at least taking the meds they prescribed for you? I don't need any post-traumatic-stress situations popping up in my jurisdiction."

It struck Mack that the top cop was mostly fishing, but he knew better than to show any weakness. "I guess at the first sign of trouble you'd have the right to ask me that, sir, but at this moment, that's none of your business." He'd left the pain pills back at the hospital, and he might have regretted that more than a few times during his journey, but he felt better for it now.

Duke didn't take his reply well. "I might as well be talking to Ally."

"She's a strong lady," Mack replied. "I'll take that as a compliment."

"Don't. In fact, I'm not sure that I like the idea of her being around you any more than necessary."

Although Mack nodded—realizing that Duke really had reason to be protective of Alana—he wasn't going to ask for his permission, either. Alana was a grown woman and whatever did or didn't happen between them was their business and no one else's.

"Did you really walk all the way from Virginia?"

"I hitched some rides. It was good therapy. Maybe if I'd started out sooner, I would have gotten here in time."

"From what I heard about your wounds, if you had, Fred might have had time to bury you before we did him." Duke shrugged. "It wouldn't have helped him to see you in bad condition, and he wouldn't have wanted you to see him in the shape he was in." He slid Mack a sidelong look. "Did she tell you that he tried to talk her into giving him the key to his gun cabinet?"

"No." Mack's response was spontaneous and he was left to wonder why Ally hadn't used that to sway his decision to stay on. That certainly would have heaped on the guilt and sense of IOUs for what she'd endured on his behalf.

"I substituted for her and sat with him for most of his last two days. She was shaking so badly she didn't want to cause him more distress than he was already enduring."

"Thank you."

Duke nodded. "All I'm asking is for you to be straight with me—with us—so we can work this out." Finishing off his beer, he pulled a business card out of his shirt pocket and placed it on the table. "But let me reiterate, I have enough worries without adding you to them."

Mack eyed the card. "That's not my plan, sir. If I had my way, I'd borrow my father's pickup and head out tomorrow. Would you have a problem with that?"

The older man jolted as though a geyser from the aquifer was about to launch him out of his chair. "I most certainly would. Knowing what you now know—how this place is your responsibility now—I trust you won't do that. There's work for you to deal with here," he said. punching the table with his index finger. "Take the burden of this place off my niece's shoulders. I take it she's told you about her brother and parents?"

"The matter came up," Mack said with feeling, as though he was about to be caught between two traps, and while the middle ground could be tantalizing, it wasn't much less precarious.

"It's not in my power to make her believe that she's a remarkable woman deserving to live a full life and love, and be loved. Believe me, I've tried. My only hope is to stay close enough to keep her from pushing against that belief one time too many."

"From what I gathered—just in fragments, mind

you," Mack amended, "she seems to be aware of your concern."

"Awareness isn't cooperation just as a bucket of water isn't going to do squat against an inferno." Duke leaned forward, although he kept his tone calm. "She broke more bones through her middle school and high school years during riding lessons than some professional jockeys experience in their entire careers. I lost count of how many instructors quit on her. She suffered a collapsed lung while in the police academy, and then the day before graduation, she saved another cadet from being electrocuted at the train station in Dallas. But the fall caused her heart to stop." Duke sat there and shook off the memory. "Fortunately, an off-duty EMT happened to be close and he saved her."

Mack didn't want to hear anymore. He desired Alana. He wanted to have sex with her—hot, exciting sex with no strings attached. He didn't want to think of her lovely body broken beneath a horse or God knew what, let alone lifeless on train tracks. He *didn't* want anyone to look at him as though asking if he was the solution to her problems.

"Why don't you just tell me what you want me to do, Chief?" he asked quietly.

"You do what you feel is right with this place," Duke replied, suddenly pragmatic again. "I won't try to stop you if you decide you'd prefer to sell. I won't even try to stop Alana from coming over here to heal you instead of healing herself—even if it gets me enough ulcers to bleed like my gut is a sieve." His tension building again, he paused to take a stabilizing breath. "But if you hurt my girl—"

"Sir, that's not my intention," Mack assured him.

"If you hurt Ally," Duke continued, "you'll wish you came out of Afghanistan the same way your buddies did."

Chapter Four

When Alana checked in at the station that afternoon, her uncle was already gone for the day. That was disturbing, since they usually sat in his office for a bit to exchange the day's news until he either met some friends or associates for dinner or went home. As this was also the first day of Mack Graves being back in town, her imagination and suspicion went into overdrive.

"Did the chief have a meeting or appointment that I overlooked?" she asked Ted Musgrove, the day dispatcher/desk sergeant, as he relinquished his seat to Bunny.

The retired Dallas cop, who in the evenings wrote a movie review blog online, smoothed his already neatly trimmed mustache. "Not that I know of. You look worried, Ally, is there something I can help you with?"

Not in this lifetime, Alana thought, although she managed to sound sincere as she turned him down. "I appreciate that, Ted, but I was just surprised, that's all. Usually, we're in sync, schedule-wise. I'll catch him by phone shortly. Have a good evening."

The trim, middle-aged man was always pleasant enough, but there was something about him that was too neat, too straight, too perfect. Single for all of his life, as far as his records indicated, he lived in the upstairs garage apartment of a wealthy widow in town, who thought she'd won the jackpot at having a police officer watching over her and her property at night.

"Watch, she ends up in Officer Ted's freezer one of these days," Alana had muttered to her uncle upon hearing the woman's gushing praise of the guy. She'd added that she caught Ted openly staring at *her* once too often, and it had given her the creeps.

"You should worry if the guy *doesn't* look at you. You're a beautiful woman," Duke had scoffed. "He probably just doesn't understand why you won't go out with him."

"It's because I have a feeling I'd have to share my high heels and best lingerie with him," she'd replied. "Or worse yet, I'd have to share him with his blow-up-doll collection."

Her uncle had laughed until tears filled his eyes, but Alana was only half joking. She'd even warned Bunny to be careful about flirting with him, even though Bunny thought they had a lot in common because they both seemed to enjoy the written word so much. Oddly enough, Ted didn't seem interested in anyone over Ally's age and, offended, Bunny had given him the cold shoulder ever since.

"He wrote an extremely catty review of the latest Reese Witherspoon movie," Bunny confided, as the front door closed behind Ted.

Alana couldn't believe she bothered following his blog. "What do you want to bet that he thinks he could have played her part better?"

Giggling, Bunny took her seat and opened her insulated tote to set up her desk for the evening. "By the way, I saw the chief pull into your driveway on my way into town. About thirty minutes ago. I stopped to pick up Louie's heartworm meds at the vet, or I could have told you sooner. Where've you been that you missed that?"

Startled, Alana struggled to come up with an answer. She'd been there! She'd been in the house. In the shower? She must've been—and he must have gone around and drove over to Last Call.

"Oh. Oh! That's what he did," she said, thinking out loud.

"What did he do?"

"Uh, go back to the barn for something, and I didn't think to look there. Did you get the word about keeping mum about Mack Graves?"

"Yeah, the chief called me. Poor guy. See, I wasn't far off about him possibly being suicidal. Are his wounds life threatening? He seemed to be moving pretty well, although he looked pale and tired."

"He just wants some quiet time. To get used to the idea of Fred being gone, as well."

"Yeah. That's tough, too." Bunny made a face. "You won't believe this—I had to check with Joey to make sure he didn't say anything to his friends, or at the lumberyard where he's working. My typical teenager son, you know what he replies? 'Who's Mack Graves?' I swear, unless I'm writing him a check, he ignores me like he does the commercials on TV."

In this case, that was a gift, Alana thought. "Okay, I'm heading out. I see Skip leaving," she said of Skip Donaldson, the other day-shift officer, "so Ed is obviously already out and about. See you later."

Once she had driven away from the station, Alana called the house. Her uncle picked up on the second ring.

"Wondered how long it would take you to figure things out."

Not only was Alana miffed that he'd snuck by her so successfully, she was annoyed that he sounded so pleased with himself. She pulled into the supermarket parking lot to talk safely. "I'm not sure I even want to talk to you," she replied.

"Look who's being a sourpuss. It's about time I pulled one over on you, since you do it to me all the time."

Preferring to ignore that small fact, she wasted no time in getting to the point. "Just tell me what you said to him."

"None of your business. Chief of police business."

Sure, and cows could sing opera. "Well, at least tell me, what do you think of him?"

"The jury is out."

Alana leaned her head against her seat's headrest and suppressed a groan. He wasn't going to give her anything, and while she understood his right, she also knew that something had to have been said because first and foremost, he was protective of her.

"I put out enchiladas for you. Did you find them and the salad in the refrigerator?"

"I just finished. Thank you, baby. Now you behave yourself, hear? Keep your mind on business."

"I always do—in fact, I've gotta go. Would you believe there are kids coming across the street from the school, planking on the roof of a pickup truck?"

Duke swore succinctly. "Are you serious?"

"More than. And it's Mayor Jim's pretty daughter Carrie sitting in the passenger seat. That's not her boyfriend driving. Jerry Terrell's the one on the roof—you want to give the mayor a call? It's not going to look good to the community if we make it seem that his daughter and her friends get special treatment because of who they are."

"I'm on it." It was clear Duke was not proud of what he was about to have to do. "I can't believe that school only started the other day and that young fool is already risking losing an athletic scholarship."

"Uh-huh," Alana drawled. "You can't say I ever did anything that blatantly public and humiliating to you."

"Remind me later," Duke grumbled. "I'll throw you a parade."

While her shift had started with a great deal of excitement, by midnight, the energy had depleted from the day like a burst balloon lying flat on the ground. By midnight, it was just another sultry night in August and the streets were empty, most stores and homes so dark, as if Oak Grove was a ghost town.

"At the rate things are going, we won't issue enough traffic tickets to pay for city hall's light bill this month," Alana said to herself, as she paused in the library parking lot before swinging around to make a pass by the churches and then the banks.

Ed hadn't even come over the radio to announce he was going for a coffee and donut break at Happy's Stop'n'Go. But when she noted that to Bunny at her stop at the station for a restroom break, the other woman told her that Ed's wife was back from visiting their new granddaughter in Arkansas, so he was probably chomping away on the vegetable slices she packed for him, or parked somewhere chatting away with his wife, Margaret. The thought brought an unexpected but poignant stab of loneliness. Just a little. Then with a mischievous smile, she wondered how Mack would react if she called over there and asked in her most sultry voice, *What're you doing?*

"Ally? Ally! Get over here. *Hurry!*"

Jolted out of her musings, Alana shifted into gear and cut a sharp turn, then sped back to the station. "I'm on my way," she replied. "What's up?" As scared as the other woman sounded, it had to be something significant.

"S-snake."

Whatever answer Alana had expected, it wasn't that. There was a snake? In the *building?* How on earth had

that happened? One thing she did know for sure—
Bunny had left Ed out of things. He was terrified of
snakes.

"Yes. Coming right at me. Oh, *help!*"

"I'm pulling into the parking area."

How on earth did a snake get in? she wondered as
she stopped and shut down her vehicle. Through a vent?
A hole in the foundation no one yet knew about?

Running toward the front door, she spotted Bunny
on all fours on top of her desk, which would have been
as funny a sight as she'd seen lately—except when she
found the front door unlocked. She continued inside
only to halt as Bunny thrust up her hand to warn her
to stop. Then she pointed to Alana's left.

There Ally saw a very confused snake pausing to
look around, undoubtedly wondering why the floor was
smoother than its skin and what it had gotten itself into.

"Now how did that thing get in here?"

"I'm sorry, but I forgot to lock the door."

Alana thought Bunny had somehow managed to unlock it for her, but she should have known better. It was
Bunny's weakness and one Ally warned would get her
into trouble one day. It seemed that time was now.

"You know the rules when you're here by yourself,"
Alana began.

"I know, I know," Bunny replied. "But it gives me
claustrophobia."

"Now? After having this shift for two—three years?"

"Then I had to *go,*" the other woman said, ignor-
ing the lecture. "Just as I started to exit the bathroom,
I heard laughter. I came out and saw the door swing

shut, but otherwise there was just a blur of someone running away. That's when I saw the snake. Ally, it's like it didn't want to do anything but come to me. I've never been so scared in my life!"

"If I told the chief that you're exposing yourself the way you are, I think he could raise that up a notch," Alana replied. "But hopefully now you've learned your lesson."

"You won't call him?"

Bunny's hopeful voice indicated she'd heard about what happened earlier regarding the mayor's daughter and her boyfriend. "He's sleeping and I'm busy getting a broom," Alana replied.

"Do you know what kind it is?" Bunny asked as Alana headed to the storage room. "It looks mean to me."

Alana repressed a smile. "That's it. *Reptilus Meanicus.*"

"Ally, don't make fun of me."

She might have continued, but she saw the snake's arrow-shaped head. Added to the brassy coloring and pattern, she knew this wasn't a laughing matter. "I'm not. It's definitely a copperhead."

"OMG! There's bug spray in my bottom drawer. Get him!"

"Don't be silly," Alana called back from the storage room. "If I spray, you won't be able to work in here for hours afterward and when the morning shift arrives, you'd really have some explaining to do." She returned with the industrial push broom. "The person running away—could you describe any of his clothing?"

"Oh...you would ask me that. He moved fast, so I think he was young. Of course, the giggling told me that much, too. I think he was wearing one of those sweat-shirt type of jackets. The hood was up."

Oak Grove's school colors were green and red for the summer and autumn tree colors. The town was neigh-bors to a community that featured an autumn-trails fes-tival and used to be part of the East Texas Piney Woods. "Was there enough light to notice if it was our school's colors? Did you spot any emblems or writing?"

"*Snake,* Ally. I just saw this snake flying into the building!"

"Okay, okay, calm down."

The thing seemed to figure out that things were not going to improve and had relocated to curl in a dark cor-ner under Skip Donaldson's desk in the southeast corner of the room. "Yeah, you're as upset about this as Bunny is," she told it. "What smart-aleck kids tossed you in here, huh? Hang on. This is your lucky day. I'm not the one who would prefer to turn you into toxic road kill."

Using the broom, she swept the snake back out into the open and, as it tried to slither back into the dark, she trapped it with the bristles, then took hold of the tail and lifted it into the air. "Okay, Bunny, go open the door for me."

Instead, Bunny screamed and ran into the bathroom and slammed the door shut behind her.

"Well, for pity's sake," Alana called after her. "I wouldn't let it bite you."

Some gratitude, she thought, continuing toward the door. She kept the writhing snake at arm's length and the broom ready to push it away from her hand in case it did manage to climb up its own body enough to attempt to bite her. About to use her shoulder to get the door, she saw someone jog up the sidewalk and open up for her.

Mack's eyebrows lifted as he took in the situation. "All in a day's work, I presume?"

His droll tone had her replying in kind. "Someone thought we'd like sushi for our midshift snack, but Bunny vetoed the idea. Back in a minute."

Wondering at his presence and whether her uncle had anything to do with that, she carried the unhappy and increasingly active reptile across the parking lot and then the street. Her goal was to reach the wooded area that was the park's northernmost entrance-exit; however, the snake clearly didn't trust her, or else disagreed, and she was forced to let it go at only the edge of the trees.

"Ungrateful wretch. Do you think you're going to find anyone else this compassionate tonight?" she scolded as it slithered off. "Stay off the road, and steer clear of wise guys with too much time on their hands!"

Retracing her steps, Alana was glad she had the time to chill and think about why Mack decided to break his own self-imposed solitary confinement. But she couldn't deny that he looked good standing there waiting for her in jeans and a white T-shirt, just big enough to make her think he'd borrowed it from Fred's drawers, maybe? To help hide his bandages, or was everything of his needing washing? White was healthier than dyed material anyway. His leather thong sandals seemed out of character for a soldier, but Fred's white truck parked beside her patrol car told her that he hadn't walked, so why not? It beat sweaty sneakers in this heat. She would be barefoot herself if she wasn't on duty.

"You do know that thing was poisonous, don't you?" he asked, once she reached him.

Was he kidding? "I'll take a copperhead over a cottonmouth or rattler any day." Her tone suggested that she was talking about wheat bread over white.

The corner of his mouth twitched, but his mysterious green-gray eyes drilled into hers trying to read what else was going on in her mind. "Uh-huh. Do you also pick up scorpions and black widow spiders to move them to safer quarters?"

"It's not high on my list of impulses, and I also never tried to lasso the alligator that ended up in the superintendent of school's swimming pool." Their conversation was complete nonsense, but she was willing to play along and wait for a clue as to why he was here.

"Good. It would be a shame to ruin such pretty skin…or to see you missing a finger or limb."

As he spoke, he inspected her bare and tanned arms exposed by her short-sleeved uniform. Unable to resist, she leaned the broom against the door and held out both arms, wrist side up. "No suicidal slash marks, either."

When he made no reply, she looked away, unhappy and embarrassed. He'd obviously come because Uncle Duke had said too much and either threatened him, or scared him with anecdotes about her impulsive and self-destructive tendencies. Whichever it was, she supposed he'd now come to say goodbye before hitting the road again.

Do you have any clue as to how wrong that was, Uncle Duke? On so many levels?

"Excuse me for cutting this short," she said abruptly, "but I have that mischief to investigate." She nodded in the direction of where she'd freed the snake. "Why are you here when all of yesterday's negotiating was supposed to get you optimum privacy? Did my uncle's friendly visit give you insomnia?"

"He did mention you several times."

"I'll just bet he did." Alana couldn't help the slow seethe that spawned in her.

"Oddly enough," Mack continued, "our meeting had the opposite reaction than even I expected." He lifted his arms as though helpless. "So you see—I've lost my challenge with myself to see how long I could hold out before coming to get you."

Alana's heart began to pound; nevertheless, she wasn't sure she'd heard him correctly. "Interesting phrasing. Interesting timing, too," she added, glancing at her watch, "considering that I still have a few hours left on my shift."

Mack's expression transformed into one of bemused chagrin. "Take that as a compliment."

"Okay," she replied slowly. She was feeling just vulnerable enough to hope that he wasn't messing with her. "So, you want to go for a ride? There really is something I have to check out."

"We're still dealing with the snake issue?"

"That's right. Just a second." Alana opened the door and put the broom inside, then said to Bunny, "I'm going to see if I can find anyone on foot in the area."

"Okay. Sorry, Ally."

"Just lock up this time."

"Um…is that Mack I see out there?"

Alana sent him a "thanks for making my job harder" look over her shoulder and said, "Looks like it. He just drove up. Later."

As she led the way to her car, she felt Mack's gaze and knew he had questions. Well, so did she.

"I take it the snake didn't get inside by accident?" he asked.

"If you'd arrived two minutes earlier, you might have seen who did it," she replied. "I was several blocks away, and Bunny just saw the back of a hoodie."

"Who's wearing one of those in this heat?"

"Someone trying to hide his identity."

"You're only looking for one person?"

"Not necessarily."

"I saw two kids heading for the school basketball court. The taller one was wearing some kind of jacket."

"What did the other one look like?"

"I didn't give them much more than a glance, but he was chunky and was carrying the ball."

"Sounds just like my favorite juvenile delinquents." They settled in the car and buckled up. When Alana pulled out of the parking lot, she caught Mack watching her. "Now what's on your mind?"

"Shouldn't you be calling for backup?"

"For a couple of sixteen-year-old pranksters? No. But if you want me to let you out, I will."

"Okay, tough guy, what *does* scare you?"

"Sleep. Fire. Being trapped." She pulled into the

school parking lot and drove around to the back of the gym where the courts were. There she saw a pair of boys shooting baskets. Shifting into Park, she said, "I appreciate the heads-up. I won't be a minute."

Mack was still taking in the situation as she exited the patrol car. He wasn't at all happy that she was doing exactly what she claimed she didn't like—driving to a hidden area of the school where there were enough shadows that any number of people could be lurking, setting her up for a trap. If she knew to come here to find someone, didn't it stand to reason that they could be expecting *her?* His own training had him itching to follow her, but he knew that would be the last time she'd let him near her. But he did open the passenger door and stand outside so it would at least appear that he had her back, and to hear enough of the conversation to ascertain if things were going okay or not.

"Look who's here." The taller youth—no longer wearing the jacket—stopped playing and rested the ball on his hip. "Come to shoot a few baskets with us, Officer Anders?"

"I'll have to take a rain check, Ty. Still on the clock. It's pretty late for you boys to be out, considering that there's school tomorrow—especially since Kenny has a curfew. Don't you, *Mr. Finch?*"

The formal use of his name did have the shorter boy looking increasingly uneasy, but after a brief look at his friend, he attempted to hold his ground. "It doesn't count when my folks are out of town. They'll start counting days again when they get back. They know

I'll sneak out even though my grandma's staying at the house, because she can't stay awake."

"That's pathetic, Finch. What's worse is that you were dumb enough to tell me. Did any of what you just said resonate in what's between your ears?"

The stocky boy hung his head. "I guess so. But I gotta have a life."

"The one your buddy Tyler here is shaping up for you?"

In the unforgiving light, Kenny's gray T-shirt stretched over his protruding stomach, and his full cheeks glistened with sweat. Mack suspected that in different circumstances he would prefer to be somewhere flipping TV channels or playing a game on his computer, but friend Ty helped him at least believe he was half cool being outside when all other kids were home.

Alana pointed to the dark mass at his feet. "What's that?"

Kenny glanced down and then slid another look at Tyler, who continued to act as though he wasn't part of what was going on. "I don't know. It was there when we got here."

"Was it, now? Well, hold it up for me so I can determine if it should be brought to Lost and Found in the morning. Or maybe I'll have it cleaned and donate it to a church resale shop. Some parent isn't going to be happy to have put out their hard-earned money and someone being so careless with it."

Looking increasingly miserable, the kid did pick up the jacket, but tried to keep it bunched in his hands.

"Hold it by the hood, Kenny," Alana directed. "Don't suddenly pretend English isn't your first language."

The boy did as directed.

"That doesn't look like it's been tossed there and forgotten." Alana added almost gently, "The truth now—is that yours?"

Although there was not so much as a breeze, the jacket began to move from the boy's shaking. He looked at Ty again, and then he bravely lifted his chin and said, "Yeah, it's mine. What of it?"

"You know what I'm about to say. Someone in a jacket exactly like that was seen running from the police station after throwing a snake inside—only you weren't wearing it, were you?" Alana asked the boy that was floundering before her eyes. "Ty was. But just look at him. He has no intention of taking responsibility."

Kenny did look, only to get a glare of disgust from Ty. "We were just having a bit of fun."

"That's 'having fun, Officer Anders' to you, mister," Ally said without rancor. "Unless we're standing in front of your father and I'm complimenting you on your 4.0 grade average, or some game-winning points—and what's the likelihood of that happening, considering the company you prefer to keep? Increasingly unlikely by my guesstimation."

Now sweating profusely, the teen all but mewed, "Sorry, Officer Anders."

"Me, too…mostly for your choice in friends. Don't let him drag you down with him. Now head on home before I decide to take you there myself. I promise you, I would have no trouble waking Grandma."

At the patrol car, Mack heard the boys utter a few things under their breath, but they shoved off quickly enough. It was somewhat reassuring to see the kid named Kenny elbowing Ty and muttering, "Thanks for nothing."

When Alana returned to the car, she seemed cool and unruffled by what had happened. However, understanding that both of their professions required a certain amount of compartmentalizing, he still didn't buy her performance completely. "That taller kid is trouble."

"He's the other half of his mother's broken heart. His father's in prison—has been since Ty was in grade school. His mother works nights at Happy's Stop'n'Go. She's doing the best she can with him, but he's got a giant chip on his shoulder." As she drove them back toward the station, she asked, "What now? Do you want to come into the station for coffee? If you're especially nice to Bunny, I'm sure she'd be willing to forget to tell the chief that you were here tonight."

"I have a better idea. How about going to the park to...park?"

Alana cast him an amused glance. "You know that's not going to happen."

"I guess I should...but are you at least tempted?"

"Maybe a little."

"What about coming over after your shift? You can fix that breakfast you owe me there."

"I always have breakfast with my uncle."

"What about after he leaves for the station?" Mack reached over and toyed with her ponytail as he admired her long neck. "I'll dare you to say you have trouble sleeping afterward."

Laughter bubbled from Alana. "You'll have to start without me. I'm going to be in court at 8:00."

"That's heartless."

"That's scheduling."

"What's the case? Did someone have the nerve to challenge you on a ticket?"

"Nothing that easy," she said, turning into the station's parking lot again. She stopped beside his truck. "The accused was caught in a breaking and entering robbery attempt. He was knocked unconscious as he attempted his getaway. He actually believes his clumsiness is my fault, and since he didn't actually get away with anything, one bad deed—in his opinion—should offset the other."

"You're not worried that the dent in his skull matches the butt of your gun?"

Shutting off the engine, Alana released her seat belt and turned in her seat to face him. "He tripped over the family dog, who's fourteen, deaf and all but blind from cataracts. It's a miracle the poor thing didn't have a heart attack from the shock of the big oaf falling on him."

"I'll bet the D.A. loves it when he has you to testify in a trial."

"This from the man who doesn't approve of women in uniform?"

"But that doesn't mean I don't give credit where credit is due. You're beautiful, unflappable. Precise, with a wicked bit of humor to keep the jury entertained."

He believed most women would bloom under a compliment like that, but Alana simply continued to watch him with an air of bemusement if not disbelief. Oddly enough, he found that as alluring as a come-hither look would have been. She was a complicated woman, bold one minute, disarming the next and always desirable.

"Let me enlighten you about our D.A., Lewis Dodge. He prefers fishing to having to go to trial," she pointed out. "Add that in a courtroom, he has a personality similar to Anthony Hopkins's character in *Silence of the Lambs,* and you can believe me when I say that the accused tend to accept his plea offers. I wouldn't be surprised if it'll go that way today, as well."

Mack smiled, believing she was finally relenting. "Then my offer stands."

"We'll see."

Determined, Mack reminded her of their agreement. "I can wait—if I have to. But what about my breakfast you agreed to bring me daily?"

"I can drop it off on my way to court...or ask Uncle Duke to do it for me."

Clearing his throat, Mack replied, "Let's leave him out of this. You know full well that I'm capable of making something myself from the things you already brought me."

"I do. What I don't know is what happened today between you two."

Mack reached over to stroke her cheek, accepting

that he was going home to an empty house and bed—a situation that looked like it would stay that way for some time yet. "He mostly growled and threw his weight around—all in defense of you, of course."

"How on earth did that compel you to come here and try to talk me into starting this fling we're supposed to have?"

Slipping his hand to her nape, Mack drew her toward him. "I admit it defies logic. But while it would probably be smarter for me to leave you alone, that is one empty and ugly house without you in it."

With that he closed his lips over hers. There wasn't any anger or frustration this time. He simply wanted to make sure that she thought of him after he left. He sure as hell would be thinking of her.

He liked how she let him direct the kiss, liked realizing that her lips felt even better than he remembered, and how her tongue accepted then flirted with his. He groaned, wanting to unbutton her uniform and begin to learn what else she liked.

When he finally, reluctantly eased his lips from hers, he found her slow to open her eyes. Feeling a tug somewhere deep inside, he kissed one eyelid, then the other.

"How sweet," she murmured, sounding touched. "Didn't know you had that in you, gyrene."

"Don't let it get around."

Alana brushed her lips against his. "I'm glad you came."

"I'll be waiting to see if you mean it."

Her throaty laughter stayed with him all the way home. It also kept him aroused most of the night.

When Alana let herself into Mack's house on Friday morning, she'd already showered and changed into cut-offs and a white, eyelet vestlike top that left her tanned arms bare, as well as her midriff. As with her best lingerie, it was one of the items that made her feel ultrafeminine. She decided that's exactly what the moment called for.

She never had gotten to see Mack on Thursday. As luck would have it, the plea bargain was rejected and the trial went forward. By the time she got out of court, she barely managed ninety minutes of sleep before she had to report for her shift. She did talk to him, but only by phone while on duty that night. But what conversations they were.

"Did you miss me?"

"In ways that would make you blush."

"I'm alone and on my personal BlackBerry. Do tell."

"Be careful what you ask for. Better yet, let me come down there and I'll tell you in person."

"Don't you dare. It's a miracle that we haven't crossed paths with Ed when you've been in the vehicle with me, and I don't want anything to be said to the chief."

"Then tell me you'll skip breakfast with your uncle in the morning and have it with me."

"As if you're interested in food. I'll see you shortly after he leaves. You're really trying to get me into trouble, aren't you?"

"*Into something, but not that.*"

"*Are you sure you're in condition yet for that much physical activity?*"

"*Probably not quite enough to keep up with you, but I thought if I put myself into your tender care...*"

"*An easy man. How novel.*"

"*Go ahead and tease, sweetheart. The important thing is that anything you do for me, I will return the pleasure—with pleasure.*"

"*It's interesting how your voice goes suede-smooth whenever I say something that rubs against your ego.*"

"*Rub away. This phone is fully charged.*"

Chapter Five

At breakfast, Alana could barely keep her mind on her conversation with Duke. Worse, she was convinced that he knew or sensed something was up because he was dragging his feet when he should have been out the door and off to the station ten minutes ago. Then he kept nagging that she wasn't eating enough of the omelet he'd made for her; and then there were the unending questions about court. He rarely asked more than, "Did you win?" or "Guilty or innocent?"

When he asked her if she was going to enter the rodeo at the county fair in a few weeks—something he usually prayed that she *wouldn't* do—she all but snapped. "What's up with you?"

"I couldn't remember if you'd said you were going to participate or not. Sue me."

"I told you last year that I was done with that. Tanker's getting too old to compete with the younger kids, and so am I," she told him. "And if you drag your feet any longer, you're going to have Ted, Phil *and* Skip calling here wondering if they should trigger an all-points bulletin on your behalf."

"I'm the boss," he reminded her, tapping his badge. "I can take an extra five minutes if I want to. Why are you so defensive?"

Hearing her voice rise up an octave from her usual tone, Alana took a calming breath. "I guess with only a nap instead of some real rest yesterday, I must be a bit off balance. Sorry to offend."

Duke carried his dishes to the sink. "Well, put this stuff into the dishwasher for a change and go to bed. And when you wake up, if you feel as though you need to switch days with one of the weekend guys because you're still not feeling like yourself, you've got my blessing. I'm leaving early this afternoon to go fishing with Dodge. I'll change at the station and my truck will be at his place."

"Good timing," she said, hoping she sounded more like herself. "We just used the last package of fillets in the freezer. Have fun."

"Fun...I'll be grateful to just bring my blood pressure down ten points. *You* be careful. I meant what I said about trading days, because we don't need you falling asleep at the wheel, or daydreaming yourself off the road—not to mention adding a car repair to our tight budget."

Alana was still pinching the bridge of her nose when she heard the door shut behind him. She wished she'd never said anything about being tired, although she was—but only a little. Now Duke would be watching her more than ever. What upset her the most was that he knew what was *really* on her mind, and it wasn't lost sleep, it was Mack. She could see it in his dear, time-worn face, and could feel his concern and—maybe not disapproval, but doubt, to be sure.

"Damn it," she muttered, feeling responsibility war with desire. She had to rein herself in or it would be Duke that she put into an early grave.

She was still beating herself up when she entered Mack's house a half hour later. She'd used her key as he told her to and, as soon as she closed the door, she heard water running on the other side of the house. Setting the insulated tote she'd packed on the kitchen table, she followed the sound to his bedroom that still only con-tained the queen-size bed, a nightstand and an antique armoire. Pausing in the doorway, she looked through the room to the bathroom where Mack stood with his back to her, wearing only a towel as he shaved at the sink. His wounds were healing better now, and weren't the angry red they were the other day.

"That explains the running water I heard," she said, feeling her attraction threaten to undermine what she knew she needed to do.

His gaze locked with hers via the mirror for several seconds before his sweeping glance took in her white eyelet vest and short cut-offs. "I delayed my shower as long as I could hoping you'd invite yourself in and join me."

"Tempting thought, but I already had mine." She

flipped her still-damp ponytail over her shoulder. It was already drying into glossy waves. "Meet you in the kitchen."

His surprised and confused expression worked on her willpower, but by the time he joined her, she had coffee poured from the thermos she'd brought. The rest of what she'd brought him remained in the insulated red tote. At least she didn't have to steel herself against his state of undress; taking her retreat seriously, he'd slipped into jeans and another of Fred's looser T-shirts.

Hesitating only a second, he accepted the stainless thermos cup she offered him. "I'm just going to come out and ask—did I miss something between when we said good-night on the phone last night and now?"

"No. You've been fun and tempting—and you still are." Feeling a bit like a fool, Alana shoved her hands into the pockets of her shorts to keep from stroking her fingers down his chest, envious that the white cotton T-shirt was getting to touch skin that she would deny herself. "It's just…me. Look, if you'd rather I leave, I will."

"Whoa." Holding up a finger to entreat her patience, he took an eager sip of coffee, then two more in fairly rapid succession, an impressive feat considering that steam was rising from the metal cup. "Okay. Maybe I have enough caffeine in me to jar my brain awake. Go ahead and tell me what's going on." But when she averted her gaze, he murmured, "Ah. I don't think you have to. The calendar threw us a curve?"

Alana hadn't thought of using her monthly cycle as an excuse. But if she had, she would have rejected that, too. He deserved the truth from her. "No, it's nothing like that. I'm just not...myself. Hey," she added too brightly, "let's blame it on that blue moon, too."

"What blue moon?" Mack asked, looking lost.

"The night we met. There was one. It's just two full moons occurring in one month, but the fanciful and romantic like to—never mind." Alana shook her head. How could she tell him that it was her blue heart—or blue soul—that was really the problem without him concluding that she really was half-crazy?

Mack studied her quietly before abruptly putting down the cup and murmuring, "Come here."

With a lump surging into her throat, Alana went into his arms. *Did* he understand what had no words, except that, quite simply, very little was right with her world?

"Does this help?" he murmured near her ear.

"This is...lovely."

"What happened after we talked last night?"

"Nothing—that's the truth. It's just that...today I'm not that person you were talking to and flirting with."

"I think I understand."

"I wish that was possible."

Mack started to gently rock her. "There's been a time or two as I stumbled through the male-female jungle when I asked a girl out, then fifteen minutes afterward I'd wonder why the devil did I do that? I wasn't really drawn to her, but I had nothing else going on. The last time that happened, I made myself call her back and apologize, as well as explain. As hurtful as that was to her, she was wryly grateful because it would have been ten times worse for her to spend hours with me only to learn that I didn't feel anything and never would."

"That took character," Alana replied with respect. "But...this isn't that, Mack. I just told you I'm attracted to you. Very."

He stopped rocking her, and kissed her forehead. "That's me, relieved."

"Whereas I feel as though I've just been reduced to being your cousin."

With a bark of laughter, he framed her face with his hands and kissed her on the mouth. It wasn't the hungry passion she knew it would have been if they were still back in his bedroom starting to make love, but even this way, Mack could make her heart pound and the rest of her body ache with longing.

When he raised his head, she murmured, "*That* is me, relieved."

"Good. Now talk to me."

Sucking in a deep breath, Alana began. "You're going to call it depression, just as Uncle Duke does and the doctors did, but it's not. I've seen depression, heck sometimes I *am* depressed. I know the difference."

"I promise not to use the word."

Searching his face, she decided she could believe him. "Okay. I was committed to coming here," she continued, trying another route. "And I could see that Uncle Duke was reading me like a book. He knew that I was about to throw myself at you the way I passionately do the other activities in my life that I use to ignore the pain, to get some temporary relief from the pain, until something goes wrong and I get hurt."

"He did mention you've broken a few bones."

Alana winced imagining that conversation. "If I wanted to kill myself, I'd have been dead a long time ago."

"I'm glad to hear that." Mack stroked his thumb over her lower lip. "And I like that you feel passion… especially if it's directed at me."

With a rueful twist of her lips, she replied, "I figured you would lock in on that."

"I heard everything." His expression grew serious. "You're lost in grief."

Alana had to close her eyes against the rush of tears that came with relief. He understood—this man she only met days ago. She could hardly believe it.

He took her in his arms again. "I'm sorry. Those probably sound like empty words, but I am."

"No, they're special coming from you because I know you haven't had an easy life yourself," she replied, leaning her head against his shoulder. "People think I should be fine by now, that time heals all wounds. But it's like a knife is constantly embedded in my heart. I feel like I should have a bookcase full of Academy Awards instead of riding trophies and ribbons for managing to fool as many people as I have."

Mack pressed his lips to the top of her head. "Ironically, I've spent most of my life preferring not to feel at all."

"A fine pair we make."

"I don't know…blackmailing you into bringing me breakfast every day seems like the smartest thing I've done in a while."

Easing out of his embrace, Alana gave him a speaking glance. "If you mean that, I have a suggestion."

Reaching for the stainless cup again, Mack all but inhaled the contents. Once finished, he fastened the cup in place and returned the thermos to the tote, inspecting the remaining contents at the same time. "I take it that's why this isn't unpacked yet?"

"Yes, well, you still haven't had a tour of the place. I thought I'd drive you—unless you'd rather I leave?"

"Why would I do that? Because I'm not going to get you into bed today? There's always tomorrow," he replied, using his phone voice of last night.

Alana allowed herself to stroke his chest then. "You're very good for my ego."

"Looking like you do, especially in that little outfit, you have no business having any doubts." With a firm kiss on her lips, he said an abrupt "Let's go. I am finding myself kind of sick of looking at these paint-worn white walls, and reading my father's old stock journals and tax reports."

As he zipped up the tote, Alana thought about how pleased she was to hear that's what he'd been doing. "Dry reading for sure, but Fred kept a good eye on his herd's lineage, and his stock has always brought top dollar at the market. You'll see for yourself now." She led the way outside. "I thought we'd wait on getting you on a horse. Let's drive over to the barn and we'll use the Mule 4x4. It'll be a little gentler on your back."

"How long do I have to wait to eat?" Mack asked once they were in her truck. "Something sure smells good in this bag."

"I thought we could park at the second stock pond. The view is lovely and there's good shade. Those are breakfast burritos from Doc's Dining Car. I zipped over there to get them before heading here. Hank Zane always wanted to be a chef and when he sold his dental practice, he and his wife bought the old train car and turned it into the sweetest little eatery in town."

"If you break a tooth on an olive pit or peppercorn, does the crown replacement come free?"

Alana turned the truck toward the barn. "Not entirely, but he does joke with some saying he'll cover ten percent if it happened during breakfast, fifteen during lunch and twenty at dinner."

When they reached the barn, they found Eberardo's truck gone, and a note on his trailer door saying that he was in town and would be back by noon. That explained why Two Dog hadn't come to greet them, too, and it gave Alana a chance to show Mack around the barn without disrupting the ranch hand's work. It pleased her that Mack immediately whistled in admiration.

"So this is where the money for the paint and plants around the house goes," he said, walking through the concrete-floored building.

Alana couldn't disagree. The place was pristine, the tack clean and in good repair, the bagged feed was safe from varmints and freeloading stock, closed in a metal storage room along with the first-aid kit and medications. The workshop—complete with a welder and enough tools to run a small business—indicated that whatever went wrong on the property, it usually got repaired on the premises. In fact, seeing the little wagon that carried the rolls of barbed wire told Alana what the problem was.

"Eberardo and Fred designed and built that together. Pulling it behind the tractor saves on physical labor, and I see the wheel has finally split from old age. That's where he is—he's hunting a replacement. This one is off a tractor from the 1950s. It'll be hard to find anything that sturdy and durable again."

"How on earth do you know that?" Mack drawled.

"I learned to drive on that old tractor when I was thirteen. After feeling self-conscious because I was the tallest girl in class for ages, I finally found a reason to be grateful for these long legs."

"I am in serious lust with those legs."

Alana thought about introducing him to Fred's horse, Rooster, and Eberardo's mount, Blanco, but they were out in the corral, and she had a feeling that if they walked there through this cool, shady barn, she would end up in Mack's arms. She was still feeling too fragile for that.

"Come on, gyrene, before I change my mind and put you on a horse anyway."

They climbed into the all-terrain vehicle, and Alana headed north to the first stock pond where about twenty head of cattle were collected in the shade of the pines, cedar trees, oaks and water birch that framed two sides of the water. As she braked, they were greeted with several lazy moos.

"They seem to know you," Mack noted.

"They miss Fred's daily visits. I try to ride around

here a couple of times a week to back up Eberardo's work, so they keep responding well to human direction."

"And then you have your own herd?" Mack's glance held new respect.

"It's a much smaller one." She nodded to the black, muscular cattle. "Fred loved Black Angus. We don't have quite the time to invest on herd purity or attention, and Uncle Duke tends to be a Good Samaritan and buys someone's stock if there's a widow or an elderly couple that can't manage them anymore. So our herd is a mix of breeds."

Mack looked around. "Where are the rest?"

"Scattered all over the place. Mostly that way." She pointed east. "Both of our properties are a true rectangle."

Alana zigzagged around gopher holes and slowed through draws, mindful of how unhelpful too much bumping and shaking would be for Mack's back. Even so, she saw him lean forward and grip the handrail a few times so his wounds didn't rub against the back of the seat.

"We should have taken my truck," she said.

"I'm fine," Mack assured her. "But I didn't expect this rolling terrain. My memory of Texas is of flat ground."

"It tends to be that way between Texarkana and Dallas, and then farther west. Every few hundred miles you get a different topography. Here we are," she said, as they topped another rise and approached a miniforest of strictly pine trees creating a cusp around a stock pond that was three times the size of the other they'd stopped at. "Pretty, isn't it?"

"It's enough to turn anyone into a rancher."

Dozens and dozens of glossy black cattle lay like the pampered critters they were, enjoying the relief from the bright late-August sun and intense heat that the long- and short-needled evergreens provided. A few calves from the spring birthing were playing by the water, only to be startled by a jumping fish that sent them running up the bank to their relaxing mothers lazily chewing their cud.

Alana parked the Mule between the first few trees. "Now dig in. I can see you're all but salivating thinking about those burritos."

Mack didn't hesitate and snatched up the tote from the floorboard. "Are you ready for one?"

"No, thanks. I ate what Duke fixed at home. I didn't bring you any of that because a burrito is easier to handle. By the way, both of those are yours if you can manage them."

"Remember you said that."

As he unfolded the first wrapper, Alana shared more about the property's past. "You probably don't recall any of this from Fred's lectures—I know he must have offered plenty—but for decades this was all dense forest. Around World War II, they timbered a lot of this region. Undoubtedly, there was a need—especially with the housing boom afterward, as the country experienced another spurt of immigration. Those pines you're looking at are what's left of the replanting. Your grandparents and then Fred worked their butts off turning everything else into the prime pasture you see now."

"I don't see any tree stumps," Mack said, between bites. "Did they all rot?"

"Heavens, no. Fred had the last of them ground down. In your grandparents' time, they either pulled them out with tractors and chains, or burned them." Alana nodded to the pond. "This is where your grandparents made your father."

Mack choked on a bite of food, then laughed. "Son of a gun. I guess they got along better than my parents did."

"From what I hear it was love at first sight. Fred was born here, too." It was also the last place he'd asked to come before he grew too weak to get out of bed, but Alana didn't want to ruin Mack's obvious enjoyment of the other information.

Having finished the first burrito, he was pouring himself more coffee and he did a double take upon hearing that. "I take it that involved a bit of bad planning."

"Exactly. There are almost always wildflowers blooming in Texas, except in the coldest few weeks of winter," Alana said, gesturing to the pockets of black-eyed Susans on the sunny side of the pond. "We go from bluebonnets, Indian paintbrush, crimson clover, verbena, to moss rose, daisies, trillium, butterfly weed… you name it. Your grandmother also planted water iris, and wild roses—she loved her flowers—and your grandfather was working to clean the weeds from the area so she could enjoy them more without having to worry about snakes.

"As the story goes, she'd begun having labor pains. This was in the old house—not much more than a cabin—closer to the road. She saw a storm was building and believed your grandfather would notice and surely come home, since he was only on the tractor, and not the big air-conditioned/heated one you have in the barn now. But he didn't come. So she went to get him in their truck. Time was growing short if she was to get to the hospital. The downpour made this area slippery, and she got stuck. No matter how much your grandfather tried to push with the tractor, it was no use, and the chains were back at the house." Alana shrugged. "The rest is history."

Mack chuckled. "No wonder the old man had such a tough exterior."

"Given the chance, he would have shown you his softer side," Alana insisted, as he went on to sip his coffee. "At any rate, you inherited some of his genes. They helped you survive the ghetto life that you went into as a vulnerable boy."

As he finished washing down his breakfast, she climbed out of the Mule and walked along the dam on the trail the cattle had worn into the already-packed red clay. The sunshine felt good on her bare skin and the sadness that had been pressing in on her eased a little to where breathing wasn't the taxing chore it had been. When Mack came up behind her and took hold of her upper arms, she let him draw her back against his chest.

"I didn't mean to make you sadder by talking about him," he said, caressing her with his thumbs.

"You didn't. I can remind myself that while he was

cheated of years, as my family was, he was so very sick that passing was a relief for him."

"Thank you for putting yourself through sharing those memories, and for bringing me here. It's undeniably a romantic and special place."

Alana looked up at him and saw desire flicker in his cool gray-green eyes. "Yes," she murmured, saying more by tilting her chin to offer him her lips.

Cupping the side of her face, Mack brushed his lips against hers once, then again, before taking complete possession. In that instant, Alana felt as though the dam had given way beneath them. The kiss was hot from coffee as much as from his hunger for her, and combined with the sun's heat, she was caught up in a sensual tsunami that stole her ability to think, only to feel. With a soft mewing sound that spoke to her own longing, she turned to wrap her arms around his neck and seek even closer contact.

A soft growl rose from Mack's chest speaking to his approval, and he brought her closer yet, his arms strong bands locking her against him. However, while there was no missing that he had been wanting this, had been hoping for it, his kiss spoke of caring, even as he asked for her passion.

Alana was compelled to yield the trust he asked for. This was too perfect to end so soon. All of her life— at least from the point where happiness ended—she'd sought a cure for her grief. Maybe this wasn't it, maybe Mack was meant to just be a momentary panacea, but she wanted it. She wanted him.

She loved how he stroked her with his tongue and

HELEN R. MYERS

113

his hands, reveled as his muscles bunched like Tanker's when she caressed him. He didn't seem to be able to keep still, either. His large but skilled hands were magical as they moved down her back to encourage her hips closer to his, then up to cup the sides of her breasts and slip his thumbs between them to find her taut nipples.

As a little cry of pleasure broke from her, Mack drank it, too, then crushed her to him, and moved against her, his arousal undeniable. The kiss went on and on, until they realized there wasn't enough oxygen to continue, and they broke apart to find reality or at least balance as they gazed into each other's eyes.

"Well, that answers one question," he said, his chest rising and falling as quickly as hers.

"Which one?" she gasped.

"You want me as much as I want you—and a quickie would be an offense to the strength and beauty of that."

She opened her mouth to speak, but had no words. With a helpless shake of her head, she managed, "I suddenly feel like such an ingenue."

"This is new territory for me, too."

The way his mysterious eyes searched hers made Alana feel he was at once moved and yet troubled by that. She laid her hand against his heart. "You're a good man, Mack Graves."

"I wasn't always," he warned her. He was tender as he folded her gently in his arms and kissed the side of her neck. "But you make me want to be. At any rate, you need to get home and get some sleep."

"I know."

"This is me being noble."

She sighed, managing a smile for his gruff teasing. "I get it. Only, sleep is more trouble than it's worth. But I know you're right." Because she couldn't resist, she caressed the strong line of his jaw.

"Nightmares," Mack said, and it wasn't a question. "I've had my share, too. That's the reason why you work the shift you do. So you won't wake your uncle… or he won't hear you walking the floor." When she nodded, he took her hand and touched his lips to her wrist. "Forget what I just said. Come to the house. I'll hold you until you sleep, and if you start to dream, I'll bring you out of it."

"We've just become real friends, taking the first steps to becoming serious lovers, and now you're inviting something that's sure to chase you away?" As achingly tempted as she was by his offer, she shook her head, unwilling to damage what she wanted to remain beautiful.

"Ally…I've seen people do the worst possible things to each other," he replied, his voice all gruff tenderness. "What makes you think a gorgeous woman with too soft of a heart has a chance in hell of scaring me?"

Alana didn't know whether she was more touched, flattered or horrified for all he'd experienced. "Can I have a rain check?" she asked, knowing she needed to build up her courage a little more.

"Only if I get to deliver it with a kiss," he said, already reaching for her.

"I don't think that's going to work."

Sam Carlyle pulled his head out from under the

hood of his ten-year-old pickup truck in the nearly empty parking lot of the grocery store. It was almost ten o'clock and he'd been the store's last customer of the day. The pleasant-looking man of somewhere approaching fifty was appreciative but doubtful as he went to attempt to start the engine again; however, the thing sprang to life on the second try.

With a satisfied nod, Alana shut the hood, and brushed the grime from her hands.

"You just need to take this thing to the dealer and have a decent servicing, Sam," she told him as she stepped up to the driver's window. "Until I met you, and your poor abused Bluebell here, I thought all men were born mechanics, or at least tinkerers. Do you ever even pull the dip stick out to check it, or the other fluid levels?"

"Gardening is more rewarding." The blond-and-silver-haired Sam didn't look at all apologetic. "It's not everyone who can practically grow a tomato in concrete."

Which was why he waited until so late to do his shopping. He was always in his yard and had the tan and leathery skin to prove it. "No, they can't. Speaking of which, I haven't tasted much of your success lately. You must've found yourself a new girlfriend to share your surplus with." She liked to tease the shy widower, who had sold his successful Tyler accounting business three years ago when his wife had been diagnosed with cancer.

"Aw, Ally, you know I haven't done that. But I have

been busy canning and freezing everything I've been picking."

"Well, when you get around to making a big batch of eggplant parmesan, remember Bunny and me. You know she loves your gifts as much as I do."

"That Barbara Jayne is a nice lady. Really friendly. Why on earth does she like night work?"

"Because she's lonely and nights can be long."

"They sure can." Sam's expression turned more quizzical than before. "I thought she was married?"

With a shake of her head, Alana explained. "Brewster couldn't limit himself to one woman. Of course, he blamed her for that. He said she talked too much and drove him from his own home."

That had Sam chuckling. "She couldn't talk more than my Maureen did. She knew something about each and every person in the phone book. She tried to teach it to me once. I do believe that takes a talent all its own."

Alana stared at Sam with new respect—and simultaneously had a brainstorm. "*Do* you?"

"Sure. I learned things about folks I had no idea about. These days when I pass out programs at church on Sunday morning, I have something to say besides, 'Program?' I can say, 'How're your bunions, Mrs. Adams?' 'Hope that gall bladder isn't giving you any new trouble, Norman.'"

Alana started to formulate a plan. "Why don't you stop by the station on your way home?"

"Why would I do that?"

Bless him, Alana thought. It was a miracle that some feral female hadn't sunk her claws in him yet. "Because

Barbara Jayne brought a rhubarb pie in this evening, and you need to taste it. I'm convinced you'll want the recipe."

He looked tempted. "I haven't tasted a good rhubarb pie since my mother's. I've tried to duplicate it, but I never do catch that something extra she put in. I believe I will stop by if you think Barbara Jayne won't mind."

"Just knock on the door. We keep it locked after dark. Tell her I sent you. Enjoy!"

She waved him off and was retrieving a hand wipe to finish cleaning off engine grease when another pickup pulled into the parking lot. Since it was now after ten and the grocery store doors were locked for the night, whoever was arriving was out of luck. But the pickup didn't head for the storefront, it turned her way and came to a stop beside her. There was no denying the thrill that raced through her when she realized it was Fred's truck. But that was soon followed by concern. What on earth was he doing driving around town when he wanted to keep his presence a secret?

Circling her vehicle, she came to his window to ask, "Are you okay?"

"That was going to be my opening line. I thought about calling you, but the urge was too strong to see with my own eyes."

Once again she was touched by his concern for her—a man who admitted he'd avoided feeling for so many years. The big, tough gyrene was doing a good job at reminding her of all that spoke to the "gentler sex." "I'm okay, Mack," she said with a slow nod. "Better for seeing you, too."

He glanced in the direction of the receding headlights of the truck heading for the police station. "It looks like you've already been busy tonight. I didn't realize you moonlight as a car mechanic."

It surprised her that he'd seen all that. Maybe he'd pulled over to wait until she was alone. "It doesn't hurt to know a few things, and to stay busy. If I had my way, I'd be servicing our patrol vehicles—only the chief doesn't want to listen to the guys at Speedy Lube grumble about lost business."

"Don't you think your manicure gets enough of a workout with all you do at both ranches?" As he said that, Mack twined his fingers with hers as she rested her hands on the rim of the truck's door.

"Oh, yeah, so much damage done." Alana had never had a professional manicure in her life, and knew her hands probably looked it. But she kept her nails short and that helped hide some of that lack of pampering. Nevertheless, it was sweet of him to show his awareness and support. However, she had a more important question. "Why don't you tell me what I'm supposed to say when people ask who's driving Fred's truck around town?"

Mack made a pretense of glancing around the lot that had three vehicles left besides theirs. Parked in the far side of the lot, that was indicative of them belonging to employees still busy inside. "I thought it safe at this hour…and that maybe I could buy you a cup of coffee."

Alana nodded toward the store. "That would be nice…in a few minutes. First, I have to escort George Lafferty to the bank's night-deposit box."

Mack frowned. "Don't they use an armored-car pick-up service?"

"This store is part of a small chain and the bank is only over there." She indicated the building across the street.

"Mind if I hang around while you do that?"

"I do," she said, using the same casual tone he'd used. She knew exactly what he was doing, and she couldn't allow that. "You'll make George nervous, unless I can reassure him as to who you are, and you don't want that, remember?"

Mack drew in and exhaled a slow, long breath. "What if I told you that's no longer the priority I thought it was?"

Was he telling her that he was going to try to stay and make an attempt to work things out at Last Call? That was…that was *wonderful,* she thought, but she still couldn't let him act as her bodyguard, regardless of whether he was capable of doing so or whatever his reasoning.

A movement caught her attention, and through the passenger window of his vehicle, she saw that George was emerging from the store with the last two employees. "Go over to the park. I'll only be a minute or two behind you."

For a moment, Mack looked like he was going to get stubborn, but with a reluctant nod, he pulled away. Relieved, Alana went into her vehicle to notify Ed on the radio that the routine procedure was taking place. She then watched the last two employees of the grocery get into their cars, and George climb into his red pickup truck. Then she followed it, and watched him make his deposit into the bank's night drawer.

Once that was done, she flashed her lights to wish the store manager a good night. As he headed home, she radioed Ed to notify him that all was well. They would now follow their own routines for the night, barring something that would require their joint attention. Ordinarily, she'd go have a coffee break with Bunny at the station, but she was hoping things were going so well that she would be a third wheel. Besides, Mack was waiting.

He was parked just about where they'd first met, only this time he was leaning against the white truck's cab door watching the road, not the creek, where the flooding was way down. Shutting off her lights, but leaving her vehicle running, Alana went to him, immediately wrapping her arms around his neck and drawing his head down to kiss him.

Mack wrapped his arms around her just as eagerly, an utterance of deep satisfaction rumbling up from his chest. Her uniform and gear made getting as close as they would have liked a frustrating impossibility; but it had been over twelve hours since they'd stood like this, and it was a vast improvement over the long night that they'd expected to be dealing with.

"And here I thought I was going to get an ear chewing for wanting to stay close to you," he said, nuzzling her ear.

Alana sighed. She shouldn't make it so easy for him, but he'd just given her news too gratifying to get into a professional huff. "You left when I asked you to, that's what's important. I understand and appreciate your impulse to protect me."

"There's a difference between an impulse and a need."

She closed her eyes to cherish the moment, then forced herself to recite, "I am on duty. I cannot tear off your clothes and seduce you now."

Mack's chest shook with silent laughter, but he slid his hands over her bottom to let her know that her words were affecting him another way, as well. "What about in nine or ten hours?"

What they were talking about involved far more than breakfast and they both knew it. "This is happening so quickly." Her fingers found his pulse at the base of his throat, and fingered the light brown hair below it. "You really meant it about not worrying so much about word getting out about you? Because I was going to tell you in the morning about a problem."

Although that brought another frown to Mack's stark but handsome face, he only asked, "What's up?"

"One of the drivers at the propane place in town commented to his boss about seeing lights on in your house last night," she replied. "These guys are like mail carriers and other regular route workers, Mack. They feel responsible to mention when things appear out of the norm. That's reassuring and sometimes a lifesaver for the elderly."

Accepting that with a nod, he asked, "How did you handle that?"

"I didn't. I was off duty. The chief did and he's been fishing with the D.A. for the last few hours, so I'll have to find out the rest of what happened at breakfast. It was the day-shift desk sergeant who shared that bit of information with me. Not one of my favorite people, so I didn't respond for fear of raising his curiosity, or by asking him any questions."

"I must've been slow to shut the miniblinds in the office," Mack said, clearly thinking back. With a philosophical shrug, he said, "I'm grateful you and your uncle bought me the time you did. But as I told you, it matters less than it did yesterday, a lot less than it did under your blue moon."

Aware of how her heartbeat couldn't seem to slow down at his life-altering innuendo, Alana still wasn't able to dispel one concern. "But what if word gets back east?"

"Maybe I'm putting too much importance in myself." He was now more interested in nibbling at her lower lip. "They could have just filed me away under Pain in the Butt."

Could anything be that easy? Not if the media got involved. "We'll see what the chief says," she replied, trying to stay focused as his caresses became increasingly irresistible. "We just have to be careful of…Walt Biehl. He's—Mack, listen to me. He's the owner-editor of *Oak Grove News*. If he gets wind of the Navy Cross story—"

"Just tell me that you're coming over tomorrow morning," he said, before locking his lips to hers for a kiss that threatened to be her undoing.

She wanted to go with him now. It was impossible to stay professional and focused on her job when he was treating her as though he was a castaway, and she'd just walked out of the ocean—a gift to his isolation, maybe a gift to his sanity.

"Barring a railroad derailment, or gas-well explosion," she relented, "I'll be there."

Chapter Six

"I forgot to include the possibility of an escape."

Mack's grip on the phone grew tighter. It was after nine Saturday morning and there was still no sign of Alana. He'd made himself call her BlackBerry because he pictured the worst. It rang nine times before she answered, and her first words chilled him to the bone.

What the hell? he thought. "Are you okay?"

"Of course. I'm just having to get out from under these trees to get better reception."

There were indeed background noises that fit—the sound of brush being moved, other human, even animal sounds? "What's going on?"

"There's some lowlife from one of the drug rehab facilities in the area who didn't realize he had it so good. He roughed up a guard and now all county personnel are involved. You probably even heard more helicopters going overhead than we usually have around here. I'm on Tanker as part of the horse unit searching woods that are too difficult for vehicles, or even ATVs. But I can guarantee you that our guy isn't hiding out here, he's heading for a girlfriend or family to get a change of clothes, food and money for his next fix. I'll be in touch as soon as I can."

That turned out to be nearly four hours later. She stifled yawns as she drove the trailer carrying Tanker home. "Sorry," she told Mack regarding their planned rendezvous. "At least the guy is caught and no one else was injured. But I still have to clean up my boy, and then myself, and get to bed."

Knowing that she meant she would be expected to report for her shift as usual, Mack experienced a wave of incredulity. She was keeping the hours of a front-line combatant. "When the heck do you get a day off?"

"Monday and Tuesday," she told him. "Almost there."

Her audible weariness decided something for Mack. There was at least one thing he could do without compromising her professionally. "I'm getting Eberardo, and we're coming over to your place to take care of Tanker," he replied. "Don't argue. You get a shower and go collapse."

As soon as Mack raced toward the barn, the ranch hand set his push broom against a wall and came to hear what was going on. Mack only needed to announce, "Ally needs us!" and he ordered Two Dog to stay and hopped into the truck.

"Gracias a Dios esto se terminó bien," Eberardo

said, upon hearing about what happened. "Eh…I thank the God it all end well."

Amen to that, Mack thought, as he drove toward the gate that Alana used that separated the properties. "Sorry to take you away from your work, but she has to turn right around and do her shift tonight, too, and it's been close to thirty years since I've been near a horse, and I'm sure I forgot whatever little I learned. I need you to help me get her horse taken care of."

"Tanker…" The Hispanic man whistled as he resettled his straw Western hat on his head. "I do anything for Señorita Ally, even that."

"He's a handful, huh?" Mack asked.

"His name not only because he like to eat," the other man replied in his broken English.

"He's dangerous to be around?"

"Not for her."

Mack listened to Eberardo as he gave a concise record of Tanker's history. Between spurts of Spanish, he learned that Fred had wanted to give Alana a pretty, elegant filly for her seventeenth birthday, but Alana had refused. She'd wanted the horse that looked like it had posed for the Trojans centuries ago.

"Did my father and Ally ride together a lot?" He had to ask.

"Until the cancer. Señor Fred love her like his own. *Eiye,* he worry all the time after the plane kill the family. One day she go riding, and some boys poaching in Señor Fred's woods. There is a shot. Señor Fred and me, we look at each other and run for the truck. Almost—" he motioned flipping with his hands, then Eberardo pointed through the windshield "—then we see Tanker come at us, but no Señorita Ally. Tanker crazy wild. But that horse turn and take us to her. She bleeding bad here, here, here," he said, indicating a place just inside the hairline beyond her right temple, her shoulder and her left leg. "But she loco, she don't know. She wild, screaming and swinging the rifle she somehow take from the boys. Bust it good on a tree. Boys on the ground too much scared to move."

As though she hadn't been through enough by that point in her short life, Mack thought.

By the time they reached the stables at Pretty Pines, he had a new respect—and fear—for the woman who was quickly becoming the center of his world. He spotted her pulling into the ranch from the front entryway, and watched as she handled the trailer expertly, turning it so that the rear faced the stable to make unloading Tanker as easy as possible.

Emerging from her silver pickup looking dusty, sunburned despite her tan, scratched up by brush and exhausted, she gave both him and Eberardo a grateful smile. "You guys are sweethearts. I really could have managed on my own, but I have to admit I'm so glad I don't have to."

Wanting nothing but to sweep her into his arms and carry her to the house himself, Mack had to settle for a private few seconds as Eberardo worked on unhooking her truck from the trailer so she could drive the truck back to the house. He used his body to further block the other man's view.

"What else can I do?" he asked her.

"Drive me to the house. Carry me to the shower."

"Lady, do not tempt me." Hearing the metal-on-metal sounds that told him Eberardo had about completed his task, he quickly slipped his hand under her ponytail to cup the back of her neck. Then he gave her a hint of the kiss he knew they both craved. "Sleep thinking of me with you," he murmured.

After she drove off, he returned his attention to Eberardo and the surprisingly short-legged black demon the ranch hand backed out of the trailer. Tired and not happy that his human was leaving him, the horse's nostrils flared, his eyes rolled at both of them, and he warned them off with a high whinny.

"Holy mountains," Mack muttered at the overall size of the horse. While Tanker had a medium-length back, it was broad, and his hindquarters and forearms were impressive in their musculature. With joints equally pronounced, the beast looked like a professional weight lifter.

Eberardo chuckled, and reassuringly patted the animal. "He a big one, all right." He clucked and cooed to the snorting horse. "You work hard today, eh? Keep your lady safe, too. That mean plenty good brushing, and oats, I think."

As the shorter man went to work, he showed everything to Mack and explained how it worked and what to look for as far as sores, scratches and swelling. Fortunately, Tanker had made it through the day without any trouble. Mack's job was to provide water and carrot sticks that Eberardo directed him to, which Alana kept in a small refrigerator in the storage closet.

At first the horse turned away from the offering, clearly not liking a stranger's scent—particularly a man's. Realizing the problem, Mack used the hand with which he'd touched Alana. Tanker began to turn away again, checked himself and then with a soft snort, he sniffed again. Satisfied, he broke off a bit of carrot.

"I can see I have my work cut out for me," Mack told the watchful horse.

"You're worrying too much."

It was just shy of eleven o'clock that night and try as he might, Mack knew he wouldn't be able to go to bed until he made sure Alana was in better condition for the long hours still ahead of her. "One of us has to," he replied to her gentle scolding. "You know perfectly well that fatigue can hamper your judgment—and we're not just talking about being behind a wheel. I often took the midnight watch when deployed, so I know what I'm talking about. Besides, I just locked the gate and I'm heading your way. You can't turn me down now."

"Oh, well, when you put it that way." Alana stifled another yawn before admitting, "I guess I was starting to fantasize how pine needles can feel like a down mattress when you're tired enough."

Mack shook his head, thinking she was too dedicated for her own good. She could have called in her sub to take over for her tonight. Even if the guy had been on duty already today, as she had, he had to be more rested than she was.

"We'll meet at the park, right?" he asked.

"Sounds like an— *Oh, my Lord.*"

"What's wrong?"

"Can't you see it? There's a plane in trouble. It's too low!"

She disconnected the instant Mack saw the light in the sky. He was close enough now that he could see more than its lights, he could see it was a small, white single-engine aircraft attempting to make it to the airport at the southern edge of town maybe a quarter mile beyond the convenience store. But something was wrong. There was a line of pines and hardwood trees that were in the way of the landing strip. If the plane didn't get its nose up, it would never make it to the runway.

Just as that thought came to him, the plane vanished behind the old three-story mercantile building that now served as an abstract and title company. He then saw and felt an explosion, which was followed by a cloud of smoke and flames that lit the night sky. Along with the shock and dread of the sight, Mack was thinking this was the last catastrophe Ally needed to be witnessing. More important, how close had she been to it?

He slammed his foot to the floorboard and raced through town, even driving through a blinking red light. It crossed his mind to call 911, but it wouldn't be safe to take his eyes off the road or a hand off the wheel. Besides, unless the whole town had gone deaf plenty of people would be doing that—if Alana couldn't.

Cold dread made his stomach roil.

God—Ally...

The smoke grew thicker as he sped through downtown, but seconds later, when he came to the intersection of Main and Highway 37 that cut through the northeast Texas community, there was enough of a breeze to thin the smoke to where he caught a glimpse of a patrol car. Was it hers?

Mack parked directly behind it and started running across the street, dread gripping him. The plane had gone into what looked like the sheet-metal shop. Mack knew that there would be any variety of gas canisters in there that could blow at any time as the fire spread.

"Ally!"

At the same moment he heard the shrill wail of sirens. Another vehicle with its roof lights on arrived and it stopped in the middle of the intersection to block whatever oncoming traffic would approach from the north. A cop emerged from the vehicle and Mack started running for the building again.

"Hey! Get back here!"

"Ally's in there!" Mack yelled back.

The instant he entered the metal building, he started coughing. The scene was a mangled mess of plane, building and inventory. He stumbled over channel iron and sheet metal, then hoses that undoubtedly were connected to tanks. That filled him with as much dread as the flames that put Alana in a momentary silhouette as she tried to drag a man out of the remains of the burning plane. Seconds later she was lost in smoke again.

The heat was intense, and the smoke gagging, but Mack fought his way to her. "Alana!" he yelled above the roar of gas and material burning.

"Here!"

She was struggling with breathing, too, and Mack

followed the sound of her coughs, until he came upon her as she tried to haul a barely conscious man from the wreckage.

"I've got his other side," Mack said, taking the bulk of the weight of the man who was almost his own height and a good thirty pounds heavier.

"I'll get the others."

Others? Mack swore silently and tried to make a grab for her, but she evaded his grasp. He wanted to go back for her, but the man was bleeding profusely from a head gash. Maybe it wasn't as bad as it looked, but he knew he was obligated to get the man out of danger.

Sirens and lights greeted them as they emerged from the wrecked building and stumbled to clearer air. Mack handed off the man to two approaching EMTs, but when he began to run back inside, the pilot clutched his arm.

"I was…alone."

Those words should have been the best news anyone could hear, but Mack was suddenly sick to his stomach. With barely a nod of thanks, he bolted back into the building.

"Get out of there!" firemen yelled as they began spraying water onto and into the building.

"There's a police officer in there!" he shouted back to them. As he continued onward, another fireman stopped him.

"Sir! This place is going to blow. Leave!"

Mack jerked free. "The chief's niece is in there!"

Behind his mask, the fireman grimaced and motioned to Mack to leave anyway. He at least had oxygen and protective clothing. But that meant nothing to Mack.

He lunged away and reached the plane, where Alana was struggling to see into the backseats. Locking his arm around her waist, he started carrying her out.

"Let me go! I have to get them!"

"There are no others—he's *alone,* Ally!"

Water was now as much an enemy as the smoke and fire, making the floor slippery. They slid and stumbled as though navigating on ice. But the fireman that had first stopped Mack appeared and helped them get out into better air.

It was another world outside. A strange abstract of noise, lights and people in assorted uniforms. Alana seemed oblivious to it all, still inconsolable in her despair, even as she struggled from all the smoke she'd inhaled.

"You both need to get on oxygen," one EMT said, as a pair of them took over. "This way."

One stout technician noted Alana's condition and lifted her into his arms, while the other helped Mack get to an ambulance. Mack was relieved to see them put a mask on Alana, even before urging her to sit down on the bumper of the ambulance. Just as another mask was put over his own face, the chief appeared.

The older man looked from Alana to Mack. His eyes were red rimmed and suspiciously wet, but all he did was grip Mack's arm before hunkering down to press a kiss on Alana's forehead.

"Baby, thank God. You did really well."

She just shook her head and choked on sobs.

Duke Anders looked up at Mack in confusion.

Mack understood that reality hadn't registered with

her yet. Removing his own mask, he leaned close to her ear so she could hear him above the cacophony. "Alana, listen to me—that wasn't your family's plane. The pilot was alone. We got him out."

She went as still as her condition allowed. Slowly lifting her gaze to his, she blinked as though she wasn't even sure who he was.

"It's true, Ally," the chief assured her, stroking her hair. "The man's got a nasty cut that will require stitches, and his leg is broken, but he's going to be fine."

Watching the truth sink in was like watching an avalanche in slow motion. Alana crumbled into herself, bending over and covering her face with her hands. From relief or embarrassment? Mack was afraid of the answer.

"Wait, don't do that." An EMT gently but firmly took hold of her hands to inspect her burns.

"How bad?" Mack demanded before taking another few breaths of oxygen.

"Amazing. She has a couple of third-degree spots, but she's getting away with mostly second-degree burns."

Just then there was an explosion that sent everyone instinctively ducking, even though they were protected by the ambulance. As calls of "Move it back!" sounded, Mack made a decision.

Certain he'd gotten all the oxygen he needed, he gave up his mask and said to the chief, "I'm getting her out of here."

"She should go to the hospital," Duke said. "Her lungs…"

"If she continues to have trouble, I'll get her there,

believe me." His compelling look to Alana's uncle supported the solemnity of his promise. Surely the older man could understand that she'd been through enough reminders of the day when life as she knew it had ended? He believed what she needed right now was escape from these sounds, and privacy as she came to terms with what she'd just been through.

As people and vehicles all around them started to retreat as ordered, Duke nodded. "Go."

Grateful, Mack started to reach for Alana, but the chief stopped him. *What now?* he wondered.

"Ah…" Duke glanced around and signaled the bigger of the two EMTs. "Steve, Mack here is a vet and he doesn't need to be doing any lifting right now, catch my drift? Would you mind?"

"No problem, sir," the burly medical technician said to the chief. Lifting Alana into his arms, he said to Mack, "Lead the way, sir."

Leveling Duke a speaking look in the hopes that explanations stopped there, he started for the pickup. It was inevitable that a crowd had collected, and many of them were participating in the new global pastime whenever something out of the norm was taking place—they were holding up their phones taking photos and video of what was going on. Then Mack saw one guy with an actual camera—probably from the local newspaper that Alana had worried about.

"Alana!" the man with glasses and bad skin shouted. "Are you okay? Were you in the building? Can we get a few words?"

While he knew he should be grateful that there hadn't

been enough time for reporters from larger cities to reach them yet, Mack wondered if the fool was blind. Couldn't he see what shape she was in, covered in soot, her face streaked by tears, her hands held near her chin swollen from the blistering? Instead, though, he just ducked his head. Out of the corner of his eyes, he saw Alana did, as well.

Once settled in the truck, he thanked the EMT, who was invaluable in also helping them make a U-turn through the crowd. It took another few minutes to navigate around other vehicles; finally, however, Mack had open road and accelerated.

Now that it was safe to take his eyes off the road, he glanced toward Alana. She sat with her eyes closed and her lips slightly parted. She was trying to breathe shallowly, but even so she coughed after several breaths.

"If it hurts too much, I'll detour and get you to the hospital," he told her.

"No. God, no." She coughed again, but then added a quick "I'm okay."

But the way she was trying to discreetly flex her hands that lay palm up in her lap told him that she was hardly that. "We'll get those in ice water and get you relief soon."

Right after that, he passed Pretty Pines's driveway.

"What are you doing?" she wheezed. "Take me home."

"Like hell," he replied calmly. "The chief is going to be tied up for hours, you know that. You can't be left alone for that long."

Alana's response was a deep sigh that sent her into

another coughing fit. Clearly aggravated with him, when she recovered, she returned to leaning her head back against the seat and closed her eyes.

By the time Mack parked at the side door of the house and unlocked it, he came to her side of the truck and found her trying to release her seat belt. "Let me help you, please." He did get the belt off her, then asked, "Do you feel stable enough to walk?"

"I'm crazy, not incapacitated."

The dull reply hit him like a wet towel in the face. Is that what she thought? "You're in shock," he replied firmly. He ached to take her in his arms, but knew how quickly she would reject that in her current state. "You may even have some PTS issues going on. We'll deal with that later if necessary, but you are not crazy—got it?"

She cast him a brief, but tearful, look. "I could have sworn I saw and heard other people in that plane."

His heart all but shredded at her usually husky, confident voice sounding meek and uncertain. "Hell, sweetheart, when I entered that building, I wasn't sure if I was looking at a fire-breathing dragon or terrorists with flame throwers. The important thing is that the collateral damage is minimal."

"Not for Monroe Davis," she replied, easing from the truck. "His welding shop is toast and I doubt he had insurance. In fact he'd recently lost his lease—" she paused to cough again "—and he was hunting a new location. Someone finally realized a welding shop shouldn't be so near a gas station/convenience store. The only reason there's still an Oak Grove or us is because the majority of those bottles in his shop were probably mostly empty."

Heartened by that news, and that Alana was speaking in a way that showed her thought processes were coming back, Mack stayed close as they entered the house. "It'll be easier if you come to my bathroom and sit down, then I'll get the ice for the water so you can soak your hands."

When he flipped wall switches and the kitchen lit with fluorescent light, she cringed. "Please don't. I can't imagine what I look like."

Mack was heartened by that bit of vanity. "You're definitely doing better if you're worrying about how you look." He did, however, alter the lighting to the one by the oven and then the lamp in his room where the dark shade cast only a minimal light. "We'll have to settle for this, though," he said, turning on the secondary bathroom light.

While it wasn't as bad as the bar of bulbs over the mirror, Alana grimaced, then groaned when she saw her reflection in the mirror. Her uniform was ruined for sure, seared in a few places and blackened by soot. There was also soot on her heat-reddened, tearstained face and her hair, which looked frizzy in spots where the flames had singed it. But it was her hands that had suffered the most. Red and swollen from the heat, with a number of blisters, although thankfully only two or three were third-degree burns.

Looking as though she didn't know where to start, Mack said, "You have to be alive to look that good." His own T-shirt and jeans were filthy, too, as were his face and arms; however, he'd suffered little of the burning that Alana had.

Groaning, Alana turned her back to the image and muttered, "I need a shower."

"First things first. Let's get cold water running over your hands." He took a stool from around the corner in the bedroom and set it by the sink so that she could sit while doing that. "Wait," he added before she sat. "I'll get your belt off. Then I'll get some ice. Even your well water isn't optimum to take the heat out of your burns."

"Mack, go take care of yourself. I'll get this."

"My house, my rules."

Although he spoke gently, she turned her head away as he unhooked her belt and set it in the bedroom. He understood. This was trying for a woman who, for all of her life challenges, strived to remain independent, loathing to become an inconvenience to anyone. On the other hand, they'd come close to losing her tonight and any small thing he could do to make her more comfortable helped him deny himself what he really wanted to do, which was drag her into his arms and kiss her until he no longer saw the images he had in that burning shop.

When he returned with the bowl of ice, she did have her hands under the tap, but she was resting her head on the marble vanity, and her eyes were closed. Mack could tell by her breathing that she was almost asleep and he lightly caressed her cheek with the back of his fingers.

She bolted upright. "I'm okay."

"I know you are." She'd only coughed twice—he had listened and counted. "But you have to stay awake. You know from your own first-aid training that sleepiness is something to watch for, as well as nausea."

"I'm not nauseous."

While he pulled the drain lever, the water started filling the basin. As it did, Mack added the ice he'd carried from the kitchen in a salad bowl. He'd washed his hands while in the kitchen to cut infection concerns for her, and gently directed her to put her hands back in that soothing cocktail.

Her gasp and shiver told him that the ice would make the difference. "Sorry about that, but the discomfort will end soon. Let's do ten or fifteen minutes in there and then we can go to phase two."

"Yeah, a shower," she replied.

"You can't," Mack replied.

"Mack, my scalp is itching worse than it did when we came out of the woods this afternoon. I'm ready to take a rake to my head. And if I have to smell this smoke and soot on me for much longer, I am going to be sick to my stomach. I know there are plastic bags and rubber bands in the kitchen. If you'll get them, I can—"

Understanding what she planned, Mack was still having none of it. "Alana, the only way you're going in there," he said, nodding toward the shower stall, "is if I'm with you. We're not going to take any chances of you passing out and adding a head injury or broken bones to this."

"If you're gambling on me being too shy for that, you're underestimating how desperate I am to get cleaned up. Besides, it would take an armless blind man to be attracted to me at this point. Make that a *deaf* arm-less blind man, since I also sound like a chain smoker."

It was no surprise that her declaration triggered a coughing fit. Feeling frustration merge with dread, Mack got a washrag from the drawer beside her and wet it in the cold water, then he squeezed out the excess and held it to her forehead. "Stop trying to hurt yourself more—and putting yourself down. We'll try the damned shower," he added, heading for the kitchen before she saw just what the idea of being naked with her was going to do to him.

Minutes later, with Alana's patted-dry hands in gallon-size bags, Mack removed the band holding her ponytail. "Let me turn on the faucet," he said brusquely. "Make yourself useful and toe off those shoes."

By the time he turned back to her, she had managed to get her socks off, too, but her attempts to manage the buttons on her shirt were fruitless. Her winces indicated the pads of her fingers hurt too much.

"I guess you won't be satisfied until you're bleeding," he all but growled, as he helped her to her feet, and took over the task himself.

"Don't be angry with me."

"I'm not angry with you, I'm angry with myself. I was doing just fine disliking women in uniform. I like to compartmentalize, you know? Women weren't worth trusting, they were good for one thing. Entertainment. Go ahead and call me a Neanderthal. I call it keeping things simple."

"Then I came along."

"Yeah, you did." He focused on each button as

though performing neurosurgery, despite knowing full well the shirt was going into the trash. "You might be feeling your least feminine since your days enduring the academy's physical trials, but the fact is that no amount of dirt can hide how beautiful you are, and your bravery makes you every bit sexier—and I wish to hell it didn't."

With her shirt unbuttoned, he began to ease it from her shoulders, only to see the flirty little white-lace bra she was wearing that lovingly cupped her breasts. Even dry, he could see her nipples through the material. Helpless not to, Mack uttered a one-word epithet, knowing her panties would match it.

"And I suppose that was a compliment, too?"

Mack ignored her. He was thinking that there was no way he could get this done without going into the shower himself fully clothed. He knew better than to trust himself otherwise.

Grim-faced, he removed her slacks and took no pleasure out of seeing that he was right about her panties. "Okay," he said, sliding the frosted glass door open on the stall. "Get in there and sit down. Rest your hands on the shelf to keep the spray out of the bags."

"Get this, too," Alana replied, turning her back to him so he could reach her bra clasp.

"Don't push your luck."

"Mack, this little ensemble probably cost more than everything you brought here in your duffel bag. It could be ruined by what comes out of my hair."

"I'll buy you a new set," he intoned.

"And what am I supposed to put on afterward?" she countered with weary exasperation. "*Your* briefs?"

Mack would have chuckled at the mental image, thinking she'd need a safety pin to hold them up, but just then she used the heels of her hands to slide the panties down over her slim hips. His mouth went dry— and he'd taken a moment to take a swig from a bottle of beer while in the kitchen. She was going to test every ounce of his mettle. All but gritting his teeth, he unhooked her bra.

Dropping her bra onto her panties, she stepped inside the stall.

When she was safely seated, Mack followed. He'd ditched his sneakers back in the kitchen. The confines of the fiberglass booth created an intimate cocoon of humidity and warmth. Alana already had her face lifted to the spray, water sluicing over her head, the weight making her dark hair like a cape covering half of her back.

"This isn't going to be the quality you're used to in shampoos, either," he said, squeezing some of the amber liquid into his palm.

"I'll smell like you."

There was a smile in Alana's voice that matched the sweet expression on her face. It and the sight of her rounded breasts glistening from the water caressing them and all of her alluring body had desire gripping Mack like talons. "Yeah," Mack replied, his own voice becoming as raw as hers. He started to work the liquid into her hair. "We'll see what Tanker has to say about that."

"Did he give you and Eberardo any trouble this afternoon?"

"He's no fool. Four hands brushing that coat and massaging his tired muscles, then cool water, carrot sticks and oats? You shouldn't have named him Tanker, you should have named him Shah or Tsar."

"He didn't have the finesse for a royal name when I first got him. That took a lot of work to bring out. But he definitely had the appetite."

"You go through a lot for him. Why cut the carrots into sticks? Why not just let him bite off a chunk?"

"It's a safety precaution. It's less likely he'll choke on a stick than a chunk or a circular slice." Alana moaned as Mack worked the soap deeper into her hair and massaged her scalp. "Thank you, Mack. I know this isn't fair to you, and that I'm more trouble than you want to deal with."

She didn't know a blessed thing about what he wanted. Heck, some of it was still formulating in his mind. "Let's rinse this soap out. You're sounding as though you're about to slide off that bench from sheer exhaustion."

She didn't say a word after that. Mack knew she'd been stung by his lack of reaction to her words of gratitude and apology. He was sure she'd been hoping he would protest that she was any trouble at all, but that wouldn't have been the truth. She was a problem, every bit as much as his inheritance was a problem. Both were gifts, too, but ones that carried enormous responsibility. Could he handle them long-term? He was a man who'd come to believe that having survived war, he would spend the rest of his life alone. Maybe he would have an occasional fling—there wasn't a damned thing wrong with his libido yet—but he'd doubted he had the DNA, or capacity, or whatever it was, to love. In a matter of days, one dark-haired, dark-eyed, devastated beauty was challenging that.

Turning off the water, Mack pushed open the door and reached for one of the two blue bath sheets draped on the towel rack, and placed it around Alana's shoulders. "I'll go get you one of my T-shirts to put over your other things," he told her.

"Fine. Thank you."

"Can you handle aspirin or do you want something else for the pain and fever?"

"Aspirin is okay," she said quietly. "And a big glass of water? I am feeling dehydrated."

"Back in a minute."

After delivering the T-shirt, he took the other towel and got a change of clothes, and retreated to the master bedroom to change himself. Then he returned to the kitchen and downed the rest of that beer he'd opened in two long swallows.

When he returned to the bathroom with a tall glass of ice water for her, she was dressed in his T-shirt, which swallowed her every bit as much as that jersey had a few days ago. The bags were neatly folded on the vanity, and she'd wrapped a smaller towel around her head.

"I don't have any need for a blow dryer," he said, running his hand through his dark ash-blond hair that was only slightly grown out from its military cut. "But you're welcome to use my comb."

"I'd ruin it before I got the tangles out of this mess," Alana replied. "I need conditioner to get a comb or brush through it, so I'll keep my hair in this and wash it again tomorrow at home."

Her eyes were glassy and her gaze avoided his, but she thanked him for the water, and he got the aspirin from the drawer where he'd put his toiletry bag. He started to hand her two, thought better of it upon seeing her blistered fingertips, and raised the pills to her lips.

"Open."

She did with only a faint expression of exasperation. As she drank, he went to turn down the bed.

"Oh, wait a minute, Mack," she said, when she followed him and saw what he was doing. "I can't take your bed."

"I'll need to check on you for the next few hours, but I know you're sore and exhausted. This is the most comfortable place for you. Get in." He held back the top sheet for her to climb in.

After another slight hesitation, she took another long drink of water, then set the glass on the nightstand and did as he'd ordered. Mack drew the sheet up to her waist, then sat down beside her.

"Don't brood," he said gently. "It'll be all right."

"Will it?"

Her uncertainty and the vulnerability in her eyes ate through the rest of his resolve and he lowered his head to kiss her. He needed at least this after what he'd witnessed tonight. Not surprisingly, she tensed for a moment, only to yield to the soft persuasion of his lips parting hers. Thankfully, the fire had spared this soft skin, and he teased her with soft caresses and nibbles, until he could slide his tongue into her mouth and drink in her sweet essence.

A soft sound of pleasure rose from her throat, and Mack absorbed that, as well. He ached to take anything and everything she would offer, but this was not the time. It would be so unfair to her, and he still had one or two brain cells left that registered conscientious thoughts.

He wished they'd grown up together. He would have made himself her other guardian, the one who would will her to see *him* instead of the horrific images her imagination forced her to relive day in and day out, year after year. He would have taught her to reach for him instead of a dangerous horse, or a career that was every bit as perilous. She'd told him children were drawn to her—he would have given her a son or daughter. Three, he thought, as the vision of a little mouth at her breast sent a spasm of hunger into his loins.

"Mack—"

Hearing Alana's soft appeal, he knew he had to stop. As she began to wrap her arms around his neck, he forced himself to withdraw. Placing a fervent kiss at each of her wrists, he set them back on the sheet. "Close your eyes. I'll be close."

At two o'clock in the morning, Mack polished off a second bourbon from his father's stock and thought it might be safe to turn in himself. He was sitting in the living room when the phone sounded, and snatched up the receiver before it finished its first full ring. He hoped that aside from Alana and Eberardo, it was still only the chief who would use this number.

"Yes?" he asked.

"I thought I'd try you before calling the hospital. Is she still there?"

Duke Anders was in a bad mood, not that Mack could blame him, considering the big fright he'd taken tonight. "You know she is. I *would* have told you if things had changed."

"Just an update would have been appreciated. How is she?"

Better than she could have been, Mack thought. But he knew he didn't have to say that out loud. He suspected Duke had thought that himself, repeatedly, while inspecting the aftereffects of the crash scene.

"She's finally sleeping more deeply," he told the lawman.

"What's that supposed to mean? Are the nightmares back?"

So even though Duke and Alana kept different hours, the old man didn't pretend that she had ceased to struggle. Mack had been wondering about that and other things as he'd sat nursing his drinks. "I had to check her periodically to make sure she was breathing okay," he pointed out. "In fact, she hasn't coughed in the last hour."

"That's good. That's very good. And the burns?"

"I've been giving her aspirin. The swelling is going down. I gave her two more during the last check. No nightmares," he finally confirmed quietly. Hearing the heavy exhale signaling relief, Mack felt a wave of sympathy for the other man. There was so much else to tend to that kept him from seeing for himself how his flesh and blood was faring. "Are you just home?"

"Yeah. Another day like this one, and I don't think I'll make it to retirement." With another sigh, Duke added, "Listen, what you did for her tonight—I'm not going to ask how and why you were in town, but thank you."

Mack smiled slowly. He'd wondered when that would register with the two-legged watch dog. "Get some rest," he replied. "I'll bring her back to you in the morning, and cook you both breakfast."

"Oh, will you, now?"

Chapter Seven

When had he decided this?

The thought came to Alana shortly after she next opened her eyes. She'd discovered by way of the small travelers clock on Mack's nightstand that it was 6:03. The daylight coming around the miniblinds confirmed that it was morning. She'd actually slept over three hours since Mack last came to check on her.

Turning her head the rest of the way, she discovered another surprise. He was lying beside her.

Was she dreaming again? Surely she would have sensed it if he'd settled down here at some time during the night. On the other hand, stealth had been a job requirement in his previous line of work.

She didn't want to think thoughts like that—thoughts of where he'd been and might go again if he felt things weren't working for him here. She had read about men unable to find work stateside, or those who just didn't fit in a civilized world anymore, taking jobs as civilian security contractors. The thought had her closing her eyes and she lightly massaged her temple, willing the images away.

"Headache?"

Blinking, she found him watching her. His sharp-angled face looked all the more mysterious and compelling in this diffused light, and his eyes were the color of last night's smoke rather than the Spanish-moss shade. Nevertheless, the emotions within transfixed her and tempted her to reach out and touch him, caress his high cheekbones, and beard-rough jaw. But memories of the way he'd stopped her from touching him last night made her hesitate. He was confusing her. One minute he acted as though he couldn't stop kissing her, and the next he was pushing her away.

He said it himself when he'd snapped at you in the bathroom. You're a complication he didn't want.

"Alana…?"

"Umm, no. I'm fine. I just—I didn't expect to wake and see you here," she admitted to avoid telling him the rest of the truth. "But…I'm glad you decided to lie down. You must have pushed yourself to your own limits to finally yield to common sense."

With a wry look, he rose onto one elbow. "I planned on doing this all along. How are you? I noticed you're no longer sounding as though you're trying to kick a three-pack-a-day habit anymore."

"Right, only a pack and a half."

"At least you haven't coughed in hours." He touched

her forehead with the back of his fingers. "Almost cool to the touch. Ah, the durability of youth. Now let's see the hands."

Alana held them up, not too upset with how they were now. At least she didn't look as though she'd spent a small fortune on a ghoulish Halloween party costume.

"Better," Mack said, his own voice still a bit more gravelly from smoke and sleep. "What does it feel like when you flex? Burn or sting?" He showed her what movements he wanted her to duplicate.

Alana repeated them. "Only a little sting."

"Excellent. We should switch you over to Tylenol or something in that family to give your stomach a break."

How civilized they were being. She was beginning to feel as though last night hadn't happened at all.

Her disappointment growing, Alana assured him, "I'll do that when I get home," and eased the sheet aside to sit up. "I need to see how Uncle Duke is. He must be—"

"We spoke earlier."

The latest surprise had Alana glancing over her shoulder. "You called him? My uncle?"

"No, he phoned here."

"No, he didn't." She glanced over to the handset beside the clock. She'd never slept so hard that she'd missed a ringing phone. Had she? "You're serious."

Bemusement had the corner of Mack's mouth quirking. "Just before I checked on you the last time and lay down. I assured him that you were stabilized."

If he'd wakened her to do that she didn't remember,

so she grasped onto the subject that served as a life vest to her. "What about the pilot? Does he know anything?"

"You can ask him yourself when we get over there. I'm making breakfast."

This was hopeless, Alana thought. Nothing was computing. "Does my uncle know that?"

"Sure. It's the last thing I told him."

Less than a half hour later, Mack drove toward the side gate that connected their properties. Alana was quiet, feeling self-conscious in her state of dress—or mostly undress—and couldn't wait to rinse her hair again and then get conditioner on it, so that she could comb out the tangles. But she also couldn't keep her thoughts off Mack.

He'd continued to be thoughtful and considerate of her as they got ready to head this way. He'd given her a packaged toothbrush that he'd had in his kit, opened the truck door for her, then insisted on securing her seat belt. Just as a lover would after having her spend the night. Only there hadn't been any caresses, and he hadn't tried to kiss her again, let alone make love to her. That begged the question—why cook for her and Uncle Duke? Until now, her uncle hadn't allowed anyone but her in his kitchen. Had Duke even agreed to this?

Hoping Duke was still in bed, they arrived at the house to find him making coffee.

Dressed in his uniform.

On a Sunday.

"Has something else happened?" she asked, unable to stop the sinking feeling she was experiencing inside.

For his part, her uncle had turned upon hearing the door open. Seeing her attire, he grimaced. "Is that any way to be walking about? There could be TV trucks already at the front gate."

Alana hugged the garbage bag that contained her uniform and shoes, and upon which her service belt rested. "We came through the side way. As for my uniform, it's here, ruined." She set the bag by the washer and dryer in the cubbyhole behind the door. "So now that we have that pleasantness out of the way, why would TV trucks be here instead of by the crash scene, and why are you dressed for work?"

His answering look spoke of frustration. "Interviews, of course. The whole state is focused on us—and they're sharing their feeds with the big national news organizations." Having completed pouring water into the coffeemaker's reservoir, he punched the power button, and then busied himself with getting two mugs out of the cabinet. After a slight hesitation, he took out a third. "You know how people are today—the crash was videotaped and someone posted it online—or several people did, I don't know. Anyway, we're everywhere."

That wasn't good news, but Alana tried to focus on what was most important. "How's the doctor?"

"Fine. *Fine.* He's talking, too."

"Well, he's lucky to be able to do that, I guess," Alana replied, trying to be generous. "Where is he? How is he?"

"They airlifted him to Dallas about a half hour after you two left. Since then anything I know is on NBC, ABC, CBS!"

"Which is?" Mack asked, his focus all on Duke.

"What do you think? She saved his life," he declared, pointing to Alana. "She was like a fearless angel coming through the smoke and flames. He learned from others that her father had been a doctor, too. Oh, the guy is an interviewer's dream. He claimed to have felt your determination not to let death win twice," Duke said directly to Alana, "and he hoped to meet you soon in order to thank you in person."

Dread had Alana turning away, only to meet Mack's enigmatic gaze. That made her feel just as naked—no, as though her very skin was being stripped off. She spun around and argued back, "The man was concussed if not half-unconscious, and there was blood running into his eyes from his scalp wound. Anything he saw was compromised by his physical and mental condition."

"But it makes such good TV," Duke countered, speaking to her as though she was a third of her real age. "And now even New York is wanting to expand their interviews." Duke's gaze shifted to Mack, and he lowered his head as though targeting who to blame for everything. "I'll do what I can to keep you out of this, Ally, but you know no one can deal with something of this magnitude."

At that moment, the phone began ringing. Meeting her uncle's gaze, he shrugged, as though saying *I told you so,* and said, "Let the machine take it. That's what I've been doing. It should be full soon."

"You could have pulled the plug from the wall," Alana muttered, and headed for her room.

"Ally! Alana—there's more we need to talk about."

She kept going, knowing she needed some time before she listened to any more. As for the interviews… those she knew she would not be doing. Not one. She still remembered the way the press had hounded them back when her parents and Chase were killed. Her father had been a beloved doctor, and her mother was equally respected for her impressive charity work. Chase had been touted as future senator material, or more. The media had attempted to milk their family tragedy for weeks. Fortunately, Alana had been cloistered and escaped most of that—but not all of it. A few wily reporters had gotten through—thanks to so-called friends. That was another reason why Alana had become something of a loner; she'd learned the hard way that there was a world of difference between an acquaintance and a *friend*.

Not even allowing herself to be concerned for how Mack was handling her uncle, she locked the door to her room and worked on getting herself into more presentable condition. She needed that to feel stronger to deal with whatever would be asked of her. One thing was for certain—she no longer felt a need to check on that pilot. *Why* was he doing this to her if he knew her family's own tragic experience? Did he see this as a great publicity opportunity to advertise for his practice?

Twenty minutes later, she emerged from her room feeling much more refreshed and capable. Her rewashed hair was still somewhat damp—the downside of being blessed with lots of hair—but it was neatly pulled back into a ponytail, except for the shorter tendrils the flames had styled for her that made her think she might like to try bangs for a change. Now demurely dressed in jeans and a turquoise-blue T-shirt, she returned down the hallway. All she heard were cooking sounds; she didn't hear any conversation. Was that good news or bad?

Turning the corner to a tantalizing aroma of onion, peppers and sausage, she saw her uncle sitting at the table sipping coffee and seemingly engrossed in the newspaper, while Mack worked at the stove. The incongruous sight had her stopping in her tracks.

"I heard the door open," Mack said, glancing over his shoulder. "Here's your coffee." As she came to get the mug, he said quietly, "Let me see your hands."

"They'll be fine," she replied, keeping her voice just as low.

"You didn't have bags, did you? And I'll bet you got the blisters wet, and the sores exposed to perfume and chemicals."

"It seemed more important to get it done and get back out here." Taking a sip of coffee, she said less secretively, "That looks and smells wonderful. Uncle Duke doesn't abandon control of his kitchen to just anyone, do you?" Certain she felt his gaze, she glanced over her shoulder to find she was right.

"What?" Duke asked. "Did you say something to me?"

Alana just smiled, and asked Mack, "Is there something that I can do?" Glancing around, she noticed biscuits in the oven.

"I've got them," Mack said. "They need three more minutes."

"I should have known a Special Ops guy would have cooking down to mathematics."

"Who said I was that?"

Casting him a speaking glance, she went to sit down, although she wasn't prepared to pick up the conversation with her uncle where they'd left off. Unfortunately, he quickly folded the paper and set it all aside on the empty chair beside him, indicating that he had a different idea.

As she lifted her mug to her lips again, he focused on her hands. "You should have gone to the hospital."

"That's exactly why really sick or injured people have to wait so long to get help at an E.R.—other people crowding the place that don't need to be there."

"More scars that you'll be wearing for years." Duke lifted his own mug. After another sip, he dove right into what was really on his mind. "At the very least, an interview with Walt would be smart." Seeing her stiffen, he motioned for her to hear him out. "You know that I don't care for the man any more than you do. His politics are transparent, he's thin-skinned and he enjoys playing God too much. But if you refuse to talk to him, instead of doing a flattering report on the accident, he could paint you in an extremely different light. Hell, knowing the way he spins things sometimes, he could end up blaming us for the plane coming down in the first place."

Alana knew exactly what her uncle was also driving at. As small a town as Oak Grove was, editor-in-chief of the *Oak Grove News* Walt Biehl knew exactly how many times she'd been to a hospital, and it wouldn't be beneath him to insinuate that there was another reason or reasons for them rather than riding accidents and being in law enforcement.

A quiet seething began to burn in her belly as she pictured Walt's thinning hair, greasy from hair product, and his smug expression as he posed whatever questions he chose. What if those questions turned to Mack? They were sure to; keeping him a secret was no longer an option. If people had filmed yesterday's events, he was on camera, too. Very close to her. Very much part of the events that had occurred. Mack was too physical a presence not to draw attention to himself. If questions weren't being asked yet about the mystery man in town, they would be soon and when they learned he was Fred's son, and a veteran soldier, inquiries would be made into his background. No, she would not be the one feeding him to the wolves.

"Tell everyone you care to, including Walt, that I'm grateful things turned out as well as they did," she said to her uncle. "But I'd appreciate it if my privacy was respected."

Without missing a beat, Duke said, "Ally…you're not thinking clearly. I'm asking you as the person who has stood by you from the start—do this for me."

Dear God, she thought. He knew exactly how this would get attention off the department and onto Mack. "No, *you're* not. You're thinking as the chief of police."

The sound of the oven opening and closing jarred Alana out of her glaring match with her uncle. She looked over to see Mack take the golden, fluffy refrigerator biscuits from the pan and pile them on a plate.

Bringing them to the table, he said, "Don't wait. Dig in. It might keep one of you from saying things you know shouldn't be said."

Yes, she thought, things were on a slippery slope. Alana closed her eyes, praying her uncle stopped talking, stopped pressing and recognized that she understood she owed him a great deal, but that this was no longer about just the two of them. She believed there was something, some*one* of greater importance to protect—a real hero.

"I'm not going to talk to Walt Biehl or anyone else," she said with quiet dignity.

Nodding slowly, the lawman compressed his lips into a tight line, then replied, "Consider yourself officially on leave."

"What for? How long?" There was nothing Alana could do to keep her voice from shaking. This was a crushing, although not entirely surprising, blow.

"Until I say so."

"That's no answer."

"Then until a proper investigation is completed."

That was ridiculous. The only investigation warranted would be conducted by the FAA. Someone might want to interview her regarding that, but she would undoubtedly be only a minimal part of their report. "What are you doing?" she demanded.

Fisting his hands on either side of his plate, Duke slid her an unflinching look. "My job. No preferential treatment."

Alana shook her head. "You've always been tougher and stricter on me than you have been on anyone else in the department because you didn't want me to have my job in the first place."

"No—because I was afraid *this* would happen." He pointed his finger at her. "You had no business going into that building alone."

"I was the *only* one there."

"Ed said he was there right away."

"Ed is full of—" Alana caught herself. Taking a stabilizing breath, she amended, "I don't know where in town he was, but he hadn't yet arrived when I did."

"A police car beat me to the scene by only seconds," Mack said, carrying a cast-iron skillet with a fluffy frittata to the table. Also holding his own mug, he set the plate down, and slid into the seat beside Alana. "I take it that could be your officer. He never did more than look at the building, even though he had to have seen Alana's squad car parked at the corner and assumed where she was. While I ran in to help Alana, he prepared to direct traffic on the highway."

Alana watched as her uncle and Mack had a stare down. "Great," she muttered. "Knock it off, you two. A man is alive. The department's insurer doesn't have to pay medical expenses for me or anyone else, let alone funeral costs, or face a civil lawsuit. What was I supposed to do," she added, when her uncle refused to respond, "stand outside with Ed and wait for them to carry out carbon ash?"

"That's enough!" Duke rubbed at his fatigue-lined face. "Ally...I probably would have done the same thing. But for the right reasons. Not for the one we both know caused you to take that risk. Now, enough is enough. You take some time off and decide. Are you going to romance life—or death?"

The instant he heard those words, Mack knew Duke had made a grave, perhaps relationship-ending mistake. It was one thing to tell a cop or soldier that they were on relieved duty after an episode that could, probably would, have psychological ramifications, but what on earth had compelled him to treat the most precious thing in his life this way?

"Duke."

Before Mack could say another world, Alana was out of her chair. She ran to the entry area where she grabbed a set of keys from a hook filled with a number of sets, then fled outside, slamming the door behind her. He knew they were the keys to her truck parked outside. Duke had seen to it that it was returned, just as he suspected her patrol car had undoubtedly been secured and brought to the station.

As the powerful engine roared to life, Mack returned his gaze to Duke, who at least had the grace to flinch. "That wasn't a fumble, that was a bungle."

"You may be the son of the man who was my best friend," Duke replied, his voice unsteady, "but don't push your luck. You haven't walked this road. I respect that you've dealt with your own issues, but if they involved other people, none of them were likely your own flesh and blood."

'No," Mack replied, "my *issues* didn't involve my own family, thank God. But they were the finest people anyone could hope to serve with. And the last thing I would want to carry every day of the rest of my life is that I'd told them just before they died that we were in the mess we were because it was somehow *their* fault."

Duke went pale. "I didn't mean it that way." He looked around the room as though he prayed the answer was written on some wall. "If she just...stopped..."

"What?" Mack asked. "Caring? Feeling? The way the rest of us manage to do so we can get on with our days?" Mack asked.

Duke hung his head.

Feeling a dread building for Alana, Mack got up and headed for the door. By the time he came outside, he saw that she hadn't left the property, but had headed for the barn and stables. Despite the hot sun baking down on him, he experienced the cold chill of dread rush through him. He knew it was empty hope to try to convince himself that she only planned to soothe herself by talking to Tanker and maybe feeding him some carrot sticks.

Hurrying to his truck, he sped that way hoping he might be able to reach her before she'd managed to saddle her horse. The condition of her hands should slow her down, he assured himself.

Yeah, right.

When he braked outside the barn, he skidded to a stop, creating a cloud of dust. There was another cloud at the other end of the building. Alana was galloping away—and riding bareback!

Mack swore. He didn't want to think of what managing a beast as big as Tanker was going to do to her hands, especially without a saddle to hang on to.

But now what? He would be a fool to try to get on a horse himself. His only chance of stopping her was the truck—and to pray that she didn't think jumping a property-line fence would be a good way to avoid him.

By the time he drove around the buildings, Alana was out of sight. He was forced to follow the trail that he hoped she'd taken.

The farther he drove across the pasture, the greater the challenge it was to navigate the terrain. There were more dips and rises than what she'd driven him through at Last Call. Alana could have veered off in either direction in one of those draws. Then a movement ahead caught his eye, and his stomach clenched.

She was up ahead—and jumping.

There was a clearing set up as an equestrian jumping rink, but a strong storm had brought down several pine trees to complicate things. Nevertheless, Alana was putting Tanker through his paces. There was no denying that she was magnificent, riding as one with her mount. Horse and woman were a perfect match in grace and skill. But the damaged trees compromised the clear space she needed to give the horse maximum opportunity to set up for each jump. As Tanker balked at the next obstacle, and almost sent Alana flying over his head, Mack felt a dread equal to what he'd experienced last night.

His blood ran cold when he saw the complicated series Ally was directing Tanker toward next. The horse might be able to manage the jump all right, but could she stay on him without a saddle?

"Don't do it," he prayed, and gunned the truck forward.

As she made her approach, Mack pulled ahead of her to block the landing side. "Ally!" he yelled, as he rushed out of the truck. "Don't!"

She had already wheeled Tanker away from the jump the instant she realized what he was doing. Now she rode around to him and brought up Tanker. The great black beast was already pumped from the run down here, and undoubtedly sensed his mistress's tension. Combined with being confronted by Mack, Tanker whinnied and danced sideways as he eyeballed Mack with uncertainty.

"Go away, Mack," Alana said, tears making her flushed cheeks glisten. "I'd already decided against the jump."

Thank heavens, he thought. Even so, something needed to be said. Slowly stepping closer, he eased his hand out until Tanker accepted his touch. He stroked the beautiful animal's slightly dish-shaped face.

"Sweetheart," Mack said to Alana, "how much do you have to hurt before you think it's okay to be alive?"

She stared at him as though she'd never heard him speak before—or, he hoped, had never been challenged by that thought before. Looking suddenly exhausted, she leaned over Tanker's neck and rested her head against the winded horse.

"I don't know."

Tanker nodded, and stomped the ground with one hoof, as though telling Mack, "I've got this, pal. Back off!"

Mack held the animal's gaze, realizing his eyes were the same color as Alana's. *I know you understood exactly what torment she's going through,* he mentally told the wary horse. *But so do I, and all I want to do is help her, too.*

Slowly stepping closer until he could reach her, Mack lightly stroked her hair. "It's all right. Come back with me, Ally."

"No." Sitting up, she wiped at her cheeks with the backs of her hand.

Seeing what the strong hold on the reins had cost her hands, Mack winced. "You shouldn't be doing anything so demanding for a few days. You have to get off that horse before the bleeding gets worse."

Alana shook her head and averted her gaze. "I can't believe he's doing this to me."

Understanding that she was fixated on Duke's bad timing, *and* conduct, he replied, "He's a human being and feeling his age. You gave him quite a scare last night—after an already tough day." When Alana continued to looked away, Mack added gently, "I'm not asking you to go back to your house, I'm asking you to come back to Last Call. We'll take Tanker to Eberardo for some spoiling. Then let me spoil you."

As she looked back at him, there was a question in her lovely brown eyes that were shadowed by doubt. For the first time, Mack did something that a warrior knew was never wise to do—he lowered those inner shields that hid his thoughts and emotions, and let her see what he wanted, what he hoped for. Desire, need and dreams—all of them calling to her.

Alana's lips parted in a soft gasp. "Mack...?"

With a reassuring nod, he took gentle hold of her hand and brought it to his lips for a tender kiss. "I'll get the gate."

Their return was far more leisurely paced. Two Dog announced their arrival at the barn and Eberardo came out, pulling off gloves. "*Buenos días,* Señor Mack, Señorita Ally!"

"Morning, Eberardo," Mack said, coming from his truck to grasp Alana's waist as she slid from Tanker's back. "I was wondering if you'd mind doing us a favor by taking care of Tanker? Alana's not feeling well."

The ranch hand quickly took hold of the big horse's reins, and grew concerned as he caught sight of Alana's pale face and distressed state. "Of course. I hear what you do last night—on the TV. Eberardo take care of things, *señorita.* No worry."

"Thank you," she murmured, and let Mack assist her into his truck.

Mack hated the aura of vulnerability that continued to emanate from her as he drove them to the house. But, he reminded himself, things could be much worse. Regardless of what she'd said, if he hadn't come after her when he did, would she still have chosen not to make that last jump? With uncertainty haunting him, he helped her out of the truck and back into the house.

"Let's rinse your hands in the sink," he said, guiding her there.

"Don't fuss, Mack. It's not too bad."

The deep growl in his throat was the best he could do to mute his opinion of that. Turning the faucet to Cold, he said, "I can get a bowl and fill it with ice water. You should probably soak again."

Alana leaned her head against his shoulder as she held her hands under the spray. "Really, Mack, there's no need. The bleeding has already stopped, see?"

He did. Planting a relieved kiss at her temple, he got a fresh kitchen towel from the drawer behind him to pat her hands dry. "Are you hungry? You barely got a sip or two of coffee."

"No. I'm not sure my stomach could take anything right now. But you go ahead. You have to be starving."

"I am." As soon as Alana set the towel on the counter, Mack lifted her into his arms.

"What are you doing?" she gasped. "Mack, you shouldn't be—"

"If you don't want this," he said, taking long-legged strides toward his bedroom, "say it now."

Instead, Alana wrapped her arms around his neck and kissed his strong, fresh-shaved jaw. "I want it. I want you. Haven't I been embarrassingly obvious?"

"That was sex—and mutual. This is different." At least for him it would be. He needed to hear the words from her.

Setting her gently on the bed that she'd insisted on making up herself before they'd left, he lowered himself beside her. Resting on one elbow, he eased the band from her hair and tossed it onto the nightstand, only to return to her to fill his hands with the irresistible shining mass.

"Am I right?" He had hoped not to have to push her for an answer, but he couldn't wait any longer.

"Yes. But are you sure, Mack? I'm afraid I'll only bring trouble and worry into your life."

"Some life." He began spreading soft kisses around her face—on the faint scar over her left eyebrow, on her chin, by her right ear and at the corner of her mouth. "Besides, I come with plenty of my own baggage, remember?"

Then he sought the deeper kiss that ended the discussion. He'd heard what he needed to hear. With a new conviction, he quickly staked claim to the beauty that had captured his imagination under a blue moon, and had teased, tormented and haunted him every day and night since. At the same time, he invited her to be herself, but also the woman she wanted to be. He'd just witnessed another side of her passion while atop a black half devil, who probably dreamed of jumps that, once championed, would lead to the stars, and beyond to the pastures of Pegasus. He wanted her to embrace him with the same trust and commitment.

As she responded to the slow devouring of her mouth, she explored him as much as her injuries allowed. Her touch was as air light as a dragonfly's wing as she stroked his hair, his throat and his broad shoulders.

"Don't hurt yourself," he warned, despite loving every caress. "I can wait until you heal."

"I can't resist. You're as beautiful as Tanker."

He couldn't help but chuckle. "Tied with a horse."

"Not just any horse. And I've never said that to any man."

Her sincerity and adoration melted away more of his

control, and Mack's next kiss communicated that with its intensity. His own hands were barely touched by the fire and he could explore and stroke her all he wanted, bring her as much pleasure as she could bear. When he slid his leg between hers, she closed her thighs around him, seeking release from the sensual onslaught.

"Yes," he breathed against her lips, "I like touching you, too. I've been dying to do this," he said, gliding his hand over her breast and then brushing her nipple with his thumb until he could feel the telltale nub thrust against her T-shirt and bra. "And this." He followed that by sliding her shirt up over her bra and then covering her with his mouth.

Alana's breath caught and she arched to get closer to the sensations and him. He gave her what she wanted, and reveled in watching how quickly her body grew flushed as desire lit a fever in her.

"I need to see you again," he said, easing the T-shirt the rest of the way over her head. "That shower last night almost killed me. I wanted to lift you off that bench and into my arms, slide your sleek, glistening body against mine. Taste you," he said, undoing the turquoise bra that matched her shirt. As it, too, was brushed away to the edge of the bed, he did exactly what he'd promised himself would happen if she ever gave him that chance again.

Alana cried out at his slow, wet kiss, and again as he suckled her, then drew her even deeper into his mouth. "Mack, please…"

He understood her impatience; his own arousal was starting to feel more like pain instead of pleasure. But having never expected to find a woman like Alana, he wasn't about to treat her as casually as he had every other woman who had passed through his life. Alana was the kind of woman to build a future with.

"Lovely," he said, nuzzling her with his lips, then gliding his cheek down her midriff, where he also teased the taut skin above the button of her jeans.

"Can't we get your shirt off, too?" she entreated him.

Relishing the idea of her doing the same things to him, he forced himself to sit up and did exactly as she'd asked. But when he started to turn back to her, she stopped him. Rising to her knees, she straddled his lap.

"Wet is wonderful, but dry is nice, too," she said, rubbing herself against his chest hair, and then a little harder, until her nipples teased his.

"Yeah, it is." Mack's smile was almost predatory as he watched her. It gave him no end of pleasure to see her regaining some of her spirit and begin to enjoy herself. Her eyes half-closed, her expression dreamy, she'd never looked more seductive with her lips pink and already a little swollen from his hungry kisses. As that hunger grew into a tight coil in his belly and loins, Mack filled his hands with her silky hair and held her still for another life-changing kiss.

Alana wrapped her arms around his neck, and then tightened them as the kiss went on and on. Soon, the same urgent thrusts of his tongue were being duplicated by her rocking and swaying hips. With a need that edged on feral, Mack shifted his hold, gripping her bottom, so he could grind her against his arousal.

With a shudder, Alana reached between them for the

button on his jeans. Just the brush of her warm fingers against his hotter flesh almost pushed him over the edge, and he rolled her beneath him and made short work of stripping her out of the rest of her clothes, followed by shucking off his.

For an instant they lay side by side gazing at each other with anticipation, their breathing shallow. Then, just as he began reaching for her again, Mack froze. With a wry twist of his lips, he said, "I'll be back in a second. I almost forgot protection."

Alana caught him by the arm, only to turn that into a caress. Sliding her hand to his nape, she drew him back to her. "I'm still on birth control pills. It's the job. Mandatory per you-know-who," she added, with a half shrug. "If...that's all we have to worry about?"

The message and question clear, Mack enfolded her into his arms and slid himself between her thighs. "It is." He would never allow himself to touch her otherwise. He had followed her into yesterday's fiery hell to protect her, and even if this was all there was to be between them—which it wouldn't be if he had any say in the matter—he would still want her to know her safety was all that mattered to him.

With that issue resolved, Mack locked his lips to hers for another kiss that he hoped would never end. He wanted to spend the rest of his life like this, holding the lovely being that was stealing his heart. He wanted to win countless smiles from her, and earn endless sighs and cries of pleasure, too. Those weren't dreams but goals as he began to stake claim on their future together.

"Ally, tell me again," he said, the urge to bury himself inside her mounting by the second. "Are you sure?"

"Never more so of anything."

He'd never participated in this kind of intimacy—talking, coaxing, sharing. He wanted it all. "Tell me."

"You're my hero. Not just because of last night, although I'll never forget what you did, your own selfless risk that you took. But because you won't let me fail. You see something worth fighting for in me, and you make me want to fight, too." She buried her face in the curve of his neck and shoulder and pressed an ardent kiss against his hot flesh. "If I can trust you with my life, I can't help but trust you with my heart."

The gently spoken, profound words were his undoing. Mack raised himself on his elbows and watched her as he slowly began their joining. He wanted to memorize this moment. She'd just given him the greatest gift he'd ever received. In a way, this was more difficult than soldiering; a gentle but strong woman who had been stumbling and feeling alone for too long was offering *him* all that she had left to give. She was looking at him as though he was all that mattered. In that instant, Mack knew he was hers, whether she changed her mind about this—*them*—or not.

Unable to stay still or quiet during his sensual invasion, Alana whispered his name as she wrapped herself around him. It was as though each limb was confirming and defining her desire and need for him. "Mack... this is so perfect. Don't stop."

"Hold me. Tighter." He buried his tongue in her mouth, in the same way he had claimed her body and began an irresistible and thorough exploration of her core, just as he had every other silken inch of her body. Her passion was as hot as the flames that had almost succeeded in keeping this only a dream. He thrust himself deeper, and then slid his hands to her hips, asking for more. His heart was pounding so hard, it threatened to burst through bone and flesh, as his passion-slick body took all she had to give and then offered everything he was in return.

Just as pleasure unleashed inside him like some too-tight coil breaking free, Alana cried out in the midst of her own release. Mack drank those sweet sounds and, together, they rode the incredible waves of emotion and sensation to peace.

Alana felt so exquisitely sated and complete, it would have been sheer bliss to curl up in Mack's arms and drift off to sleep—except that she couldn't stop exploring and stroking him. She loved his body—even his scars, because they were evidence of how he had cheated death. Now that he was resting and healing—and probably eating more—his muscles showed greater definition. Dressed, Mack was impressive and intimidating, naked he made her mouth water.

"From now on, whenever I see you pampering Tanker, I'm going to be jealous as hell," he drawled, under her self-indulgent exploration.

He was lying with his eyes closed, and he spoke with a deceptive laziness, but the moment he slid his hand down her back, all the way to where they were still joined, she knew he wasn't anything close to sleepy.

After a soft whimper as he brought her impossibly close to ecstasy again, she pressed a kiss into the soft mat of hair over his heart.

"You have nothing to be jealous of. I'm willing to do this any and every time you'll let me." As she helplessly tightened muscles inside in order to enjoy every last bit of him, she moaned softly. "Thank you."

He lifted his lids only enough to see her beneath lashes that were shades darker than his hair. "Any and all thanks are mine, darling."

"No. You make me feel—more than I ever have. More than winning those competitions or graduating with honors from the academy, or..."

As her voice drifted off, Mack's turned into a wicked grin. "On second thought, I'll take that last 'or.'" But just as quickly, his expression grew serious and he tightened his arms around her. "Stay with me."

She knew what he was saying. "I want to." She wasn't ready to return to the house, anyway.

"Call your uncle."

"Maybe. Later." Still stinging from his behavior, Alana explained, "I don't want to listen to any more *orders*. He's the one who forced leave on me."

"At least tell him where you are."

"As if he doesn't know? I suspect as soon as he arrived at the crash scene and discovered you'd beat him, he had to draw some conclusions."

Mack's gray-green eyes lit with secret humor. "You're right. I've been as subtle about my intentions as a meteor landing in his kitchen." Then he added quietly, "You are the bravest woman I've ever met. He's a wrung-out cop short on sleep, who almost lost the last member of his family yesterday—the niece he adores, when he's thinking straight. You can't be afraid to talk to that man."

Alana wished she could make light of that, but this was too serious a matter. "I'm afraid of what else he's likely to ask of me—or that he'll keep heaping on the guilt. I'm grateful to him for a great deal, don't get me wrong, but I've never failed to pull my weight on the force."

"I never suspected otherwise."

With a sigh, she settled her chin on his chest, doubt creeping into her mind nonetheless. "Was I wrong to refuse the interview with Walt?"

"Not if you believe he would bring up too much that's painful about your past. From the way Duke described him, he doesn't sound like a guy who plays fair."

"It's not only that," she replied. "I don't want any of this to bring you into the dialogue, and I just know it would."

Mack took hold of one of her hands, his gaze concerned as he studied the wounds. "We're together, Alana. I can't help but become part of that dialogue. The challenge will be to deal with things on our terms."

As he kissed each injured finger, Alana felt her heart constrict. "But what about your own situation? By now, half the town must know Fred Graves's only son is back in town, and at least a few of them are surfing the web trying to find out what you've been doing all this time. That could trigger alarms in certain places."

"I'm a reluctant medal recipient, not one of America's Ten Most Wanted."

"Which is so insignificant that you tried to blackmail me into keeping your identity a secret in order to agree to stay here?"

Mack slid his hands to her bottom and lifted his hips against hers, making it impossible for her not to feel that he wanted her again. "I was buying myself time with you, so I could figure out if you were half as sweetly noble as you were tantalizing. And guess what I discovered?" he asked, drawing her up to claim her lips.

Chapter Eight

"You know I'm not going to ask."

It was Monday morning—almost lunchtime—and Mack came through the door looking as though he'd just stepped outside for a moment when, in fact, he'd been gone since shortly after she'd wakened and stepped into the shower. Once she'd emerged, she'd discovered, in rather slow process, that he was nowhere to be found. Fred's white pickup was gone. Mack's empty coffee mug was in the sink, and his billfold was missing from where he'd set it last night.

Finally, she'd gone back to the bedroom to find a note saying *Back by noon. You still take my breath away with or without the frosted glass between us.*

At the time, she'd been moved by that romantic gesture, but not now. Now she was thinking, *Sneak,* as he started to smile and look all too pleased with himself. She had just returned from caring for Tanker next door, and didn't want to think about how handsome he looked in his black short-sleeved shirt and jeans. To stay busy, she continued to get ingredients for a salad out of the vegetable bin in the refrigerator. But inside, she was falling apart.

What had he done? Where had he gone?

Mack set his keys on the kitchen table and came behind her as she set the last items on the counter. Wrapping his tanned arms around her waist, he nuzzled the side of her neck. "I missed you, too. God, you smell good enough to eat, and you feel even better."

They had been together nonstop since Saturday. It had been a fantasy world where they made love, cooked, made love, talked and made love again. He'd helped her with Tanker and the herd, then they'd both worked with Eberardo to tend to Fred's mount, Rooster, and Eberardo's Blanco. She'd sensed Mack was almost ready to hone the riding skills he'd only begun to learn as a child, and she looked forward to the day when they could ride around their properties together. But his unanticipated disappearance threatened to burst that happy daydream.

Unable to maintain her offended demeanor, Alana twisted around so she could wrap her arms around him. "Damn it, Mack—you worried me."

"I left you a note." He stroked her back and pressed her against the cabinets, suggestively rubbing his hips against hers to let her know how quickly she got to him. "I was inspired."

"If you'd stayed, you would have seen me blush."

Desire triggered green fire in his eyes. "If I'd stayed, the well would have run dry."

Laughing despite her concern, Alana gave him a kiss meant to show him that she would have enjoyed at least trying for that. She couldn't help herself. He was changing her life, and giving her hope. What he was doing was making her fall deeper and deeper in love with him.

With an appreciative groan, Mack tightened his arms and kissed her back. By the time he lifted his head to gaze into her eyes, she was ready to delay lunch.

"Are you okay?" she asked, searching his ruggedly handsome face for the truth.

"I am. By the way, your uncle sends his love."

"You went to go see Uncle Duke? At the station?" Although Alana had called her uncle on Sunday, as Mack had urged, she had otherwise kept her distance, needing more time to come to terms with things. Ultimately, she loved Duke and would forgive him, but she didn't know if she could continue to work for him. In fact, she didn't know if she still wanted to be in law enforcement, either.

"No, but our paths crossed," Mack said, his gaze admiring as he took in her lavender blouse and white shorts.

"So you were in town?" Alana knew that he felt that it was time to rejoin the community, but she was feeling selfish and wanted him to herself for a while longer.

"Part of the time."

What on earth was going on with these cryptic replies? Where else could he have gone? Tyler? Longview? He'd been gone long enough, but for what reason?

"I sat down with Walt Biehl, sweetheart."

"No!" Alana fisted her hands against Mack's chest, only to realize she'd also filled her hands with his shirt. With a flustered shake of her head, she smoothed the material and struggled to continue with a calmer voice. "Mack, that was such a mistake. Why did you do that?"

"So that you wouldn't have to. That was my deal with him." He kissed her forehead and held her close, rocking her gently, clearly willing her to adjust to the idea.

"And you said I'm too brave for my own good?"

"It was worth it—especially once I'd made the decision that it was the best thing for us."

Us. Alana couldn't help but thrill at hearing him say that. But she worried still. "How bad was it? Please don't tell me you told him about how you earned your medal when you haven't even told me?"

"No, that was my other condition." Framing her face with his hands, Mack forced her to meet his gaze. "The point is that there's been enough state and nationwide news to push your heroism far enough behind other stories. That diminished Walt's argument that he had 'first dibs' on at least one of the two scoops he'd been aiming for."

That would be wonderful news, except for the story Walt had still wanted. "The worm. How bad was it?"

"I've been through worse" was Mack's conservative reply.

Alana shook her head, knowing what he was doing. She'd have to read the damned article herself to know what Walt had wheedled and negotiated out of him.

And Mack had done this so that she wouldn't have to. Dear God, was there no end to this man's nobleness?

"You frustrating, sweet man! Thank you," she added softly. She kissed him tenderly, only to be crushed against him as he turned the kiss into a seduction that left her clinging to him.

She should have guessed what he'd been doing. The potential for it had been in his every look and touch since he coaxed her to join him here at Last Call. And there had been other benefits to his attentiveness— she'd actually been sleeping more, and had only had one bad dream, which Mack had quickly brought her out of, soon convincing her to focus on other things. Him!

"I found some shrimp in the freezer and planned to make us a shrimp salad for lunch," she told him, nuzzling his jaw and the side of his neck. "I thought if I fixated on pampering you as much as I just did Tanker, that would ESP you wherever you were and you'd come back."

"It worked, didn't it?" he mused, fixating himself, as he caressed her hips. "Did I happen to mention that it should be illegal for you to wear shorts anywhere but in here with me?"

With a brief, breathless laugh, Alana tried to lose herself in his caresses, but something kept nagging at her. "Mack…what am I missing? Correction, what aren't you telling me?" There was something. She could feel it like a tiny fruit fly buzzing around her head.

He paused, only to exhale and lean his forehead against hers. "You were supposed to let me make love to you first, so that you'd be replete and accepting when I told you."

Despite the inviting images, an invisible fist clenched Alana's heart. "Tell me."

"I'm going back."

All she saw was vast space, thousands of miles between them. Bad rides on worn-out airplanes. A shortage of supplies on the battlefield. Unbearable cold. Unbearable heat. Loneliness. Danger.

"Alana, love…I meant only back to Virginia to deal with the damned medal."

For a second, she couldn't breathe as emotion strangled her. Then, abruptly, she started to sob. She didn't know whether it was from soul-deep relief, or too much dread at the thought of having to put up a stoic front as he returned to doing what he thought was all that he was good at. Of course, if that's what he asked of her, she would have somehow managed, she knew that as well as she knew she could never be with anyone else but him. He'd not only won that commitment from her, he'd earned it by selflessly being there for her.

"Ally. Baby."

"Sorry. Sorry. I don't know where that's coming from."

Without a word, Mack lifted her into his arms and carried her to the shadowy room where they'd shared heaven for two days and nights. Laying her on the neatly turned covers where blues and greens created a pool of cool serenity, he wrapped her into his arms.

"Do you know what it does to me to know you care that much? Ally…it's the same for me."

As he stroked her hair, she searched his face. The green and silver fire she saw flickering in his eyes wasn't only desire. Maybe he couldn't say the words yet; after a childhood where he'd endured a dreadful deprivation of human kindness, let alone love, it was natural for him not to recognize it when it was being offered to him body and soul. So she would show him with every breath in her body, until he believed.

"I'm here, sweetheart," he assured her. "This is home from here on, regardless of what happens."

"I'm so glad," she whispered, needing to get closer. She kissed him as he had her, with a gently fierce need that could have only one ending.

With a soft groan, Mack rolled onto his back and drew her over him, cupping and caressing her hips and rocking her against him. Then he slid his hands up to the outer swells of her breasts, and back down again in an urgent attempt to soothe as much as possess.

Alana felt the same eagerness and plucked at the buttons of his shirt in order to touch more of him and feel his heart race beneath her lips. Despite the cool, air-conditioned room, his body grew feverish and damp under her roaming fingers. But it was her soft bites and kittenlike licks that soon pulled another guttural sound from him.

"Do you know how crazy that makes me?" he asked, stroking her hair. "I go to sleep still feeling your mouth on me. I wake up praying for your mouth on me. I dream of that sweet mouth on me."

As Alana unbuttoned and unzipped his jeans, she whispered, "Good. Because I love the taste of you."

This was the man she wished had been her first lover. She'd never felt freer to be herself or more desirable. However, before she'd barely begun to bring him the pleasure he'd shown her, Mack drew her back up into his arms, his entire body tight with anticipation.

"Kiss me," he said, his hands already busy removing the last barriers of clothing between them. As she immediately offered him her mouth, he slid his hand into her opened shorts and beneath her panties, until he found her warm, moist center and beyond.

The sensations drew a gasp from her and she closed her thighs around his hand. "Oh, Mack…it'll be over too soon."

"I want to watch. I love being able to make you lose control."

And she did. Riding and writhing the hand that was performing exquisite torture on her, she soared quickly to a sharp climax, and that had her crying his name and clutching his shoulders. Then, shuddering, she buried her face against his neck, tasting him as she waited to regain control of her love-weakened body.

"I bet you're proud of yourself," she murmured, rubbing her cheek against his before meeting his intent gaze and wholly masculine smile.

"I am," he replied, already starting to free her from the rest of her clothes.

His gaze was dark and possessive as he swept his hand down her body, before rolling onto his back and lifting her over him. It didn't surprise her that this was the most natural position for her; she'd loved the unique feeling of freedom and control since she climbed on her

first pony at the age of three. But maturity definitely
had its benefits, she thought, as she slowly took Mack
into her body.

"That is one mischievous smile," Mack noted, his
voice sounding like a big cat purring.

"I was just thinking how wonderful it is that we
like the same things." As she began a languid rocking,
as though taking Tanker on a lazy morning ride, their
eyes met and held.

"Wonderful," he murmured, filling his hands with
her breasts, then caressing her with his thumbs, until
her nipples hardened and pebbled. "And I have the better view."

Alana would challenge that, but the words locked
in her throat, as Mack shifted his hold to her hips to
encourage her to take him deeper. She loved watching
his face as focus and desire battled: his eyes growing
low-hooded, a muscle in his cheek flexing as he ground
his teeth together, his Adam's apple rising and falling.
She would be terrified of him and for him on a battlefield, but here she'd never felt safer or more cherished.

"Don't stop, Mack. It's too perfect."

He didn't. He only made things better, as his thumb
sought and found the nub that would compel her to find
release again, and propel him to his.

As he did climax, he drew her down to him for a
slightly desperate kiss that peaked as they drank each
other's cries of completion.

"Come with me."

Alana had been lying in Mack's arms as still as if

she'd drifted off to sleep, but Mack knew she wasn't. Like him she was just relishing the aftereffects of them finding a new truth and closeness with each other.

Stroking the delicate line of her jaw, he added, "It will be easier for me to do this if I can have you there."

That had her lifting her eyelids, albeit reluctantly. Mack understood; she was afraid for him. Beneath her dark, dense lashes, her brown eyes gauged his seriousness.

"I don't want you to go. Now you're asking me to be an accessory to...I don't know what."

"It's not like they're going to lock me up."

"Really? You know this?" Alana rolled onto her tummy, and studied him with aching concern. "You walk out of the hospital claiming to have signed enough papers to make that okay, but you were undoubtedly on pain medication, so how do you know for sure? They may have you listed as AWOL or something."

"I'd weaned myself off most of the meds," he replied patiently, "and flushed the things down the commode. There may be goldfish and baby alligators swimming in the sewer system feeling no pain, but I was done with being turned into a pill popper."

"Oh, that's reassuring," Alana muttered, although she returned to playing with his chest hairs. "You decided to walk across the *country* with a *clear* head. You could have overdone it. You could have injured yourself and internally bled. Died!"

"But I didn't. Instead, I found you."

Although her tempting lips were fighting a smile,

she amended, "So much for your clear head, mister. I'm the one who found *you*."

And now he didn't want to be without her even for one day. "Duke is making you take some time. A change of scenery might do you a world of good." Unable to resist temptation, he brushed his thumb over her nipple, despite knowing he wasn't playing fair. But then he was playing for keeps.

"When was the last time you left Oak Grove?"

"College," she admitted, arching into his caress. "But it was in Texas, so that doesn't exactly count. And the academy was in Dallas."

"So it's time you see what's beyond the Lone Star State's borders and on the other side of the Mississippi." He wanted a chance to spoil her a little. Wine her, dine her—and show her off. They hadn't even had a proper first date yet!

"You know we'd be asking a lot of Eberardo to watch over both properties," Alana said with some concern.

"I'll give him a raise and tell him to hire someone to help him. This place alone can handle that." His study of his father's accounts showed that the old guy had been tightfisted, and while that wasn't a bad thing, there were repairs and improvements to be made, and he needed time for that, so he wouldn't always be available to be out helping Eberardo. Mack also had his own money— and his own plans. One included keeping Alana way too busy to do all the work she was handling herself. "Do you think he'd go for that idea? If he's serious about that nurse you were telling me about, he needs a little corner of land of his own for that trailer of his. Or better yet, the new hand could take it over and I'd help him build a house or something."

"Mack!" Alana kissed him with a girlish enthusiasm. "That's wonderful news! He'll be so grateful and proud. It's been so important for him to show you how dependable and trustworthy he is."

"I can see that he is." But Mack circled back to his main priority. "So does that mean you'll come with me?"

She raked her teeth over her lower lip. "I'll have to talk to Uncle Duke, although I suspect he'll take all of thirty seconds to pack my suitcase and hand it to you."

"No, he won't," Mack replied, adding smoothly, "but I'd take it." He watched her struggle with temptation and her sense of responsibility.

"When do you think we'd leave?" she asked.

"I have calls to make. But I'm guessing in a week, or two at the most. We can take our time driving up, and coming back. I thought I'd rent a car, so it will really feel like a vacation."

Looking bemused, Alana eyed him with increased speculation. "You've been giving this some thought."

Tracing his fingers down the seductive dip at the small of her back, he asked, "Want a preview of things to come?"

"*That's* the Mississippi River?"

Staring through the passenger window of the Cadillac Mack had rented, Ally thought of her romantic vision inspired by her schoolgirl readings of Mark Twain. There were no shorelines with trees draped with Span-

ish moss, no paddle boat in sight, or fishermen holding cane poles as they concentrated on trying to catch
dinner. Old Man River was really a mud slick with
some equally dirty and rusting barges cutting through
it. Once she did spot one or two fisherman, she was
concerned for their health. She would never want to eat
anything they brought out of that water.

"Disappointed?"

Trying to be positive, she said diplomatically, "It's
been raining pretty heavily to the north. I'm sure that
has something to do with conditions."

"So does constant dredging." Mack reached over
and gently touched her hands that were almost healed.
"Are you hungry yet?"

It wasn't quite two weeks since Alana had agreed to
come with him on this journey, and they'd been on the
road since dawn driving in the black sedan that Mack
had decided would be wiser for the trip. Fred's truck
had plenty of miles on it. Besides, Mack had explained
to her, a comfortable sedan with all of the bells and
whistles was more romantic. Who was she to argue?

"I think I'm still digesting that big breakfast you
bought me in Texarkana," she teased.

Alana knew she'd worried him for a while that she
might back out at the last minute. Nervous to be leaving
Tanker to Eberardo and the new hand, Antonio, she'd
snuck over to the stable at Pretty Pines before their de-
parture to bring Tanker an apple. Her uncle must have
spotted her truck lights and came to give her a last hug.

"You'll have a good time," Duke said, his voice gruff

and his hug almost fierce. The words were an order, not a question.

"I mean to try. I trust Eberardo to take good care of things in here, but it's been several years since we've been apart for more than a few hours. Please take a moment to bring Tanker an apple or carrot once a day? He'll get lonely."

"Some lapdog you raised." But Duke had gone soft as he eyed her white-and-black sundress. "Don't you look like something to buy at the bakery? Is that new?"

"I can't face the secretary of the navy in blue jeans," she replied, knowing first and foremost she'd shopped to make Mack proud of her. "Will you tell Bunny I'm sorry for abandoning her, too? Is she getting on okay with just Ed there on the evening shift?"

"Funny thing is that she has company most nights— at least until almost midnight."

"Sam? Sam Carlyle has been keeping company with Barbara Jayne?"

"That's the word going around."

How wonderful for both of them, Alana thought. It had been sheer impulse to bring those two together. Now with more miles between here and home, and her cell phone remaining quiet, she was starting to believe she just might be able to relax and enjoy herself. At least until they arrived in Virginia.

"Hey, daydreamer."

Mack's voice drew Alana back to the present. "Sorry, did you ask me something?"

"How far do you want to go tonight?" he asked her.

"You're driving. How tired are you?" Remembering the other reason he wanted a vehicle with the best seating, she asked quickly, "Is your back okay? Do you need me to take over?"

"I'm a little stiff, which I'd be complaining about anyway after all these hours in one position. Why don't we pull off now and look around Memphis? I took a quick glimpse on my way down to Texas, and thought I'd like to check it out again. You've never even told me if you like music, and what kind. Some of the biggest names in rock and roll and the blues are linked to this city—Elvis, Jerry Lee, Johnny Cash—"

"I loved his voice. His country-western ballads…"

"Nobody did them better," Mack agreed, "but he did a Nine Inch Nails song called 'Hurt' that gets me right in the gut every time I hear it. That man could cross all genres because he respected them all."

"I have that song on a CD. It's incredibly moving." Alana studied his profile. "Is this where I learn that you're a closet musician?"

"No way," Mack replied. "Can't play any instrument or carry a note to save my life. But there's nothing like being on the other side of the world and hearing a song you wrinkled your nose at when you were a kid and suddenly it's like hearing it for the first time—and sometimes it's like the singer wrote it with exactly you in mind."

Alana stroked his shoulder. "I wish we knew each other sooner. I would have written you during deployments, and sent you care packages."

Mack shook his head, his smile wry. "Sweetheart, if you were in my life then, I would probably be sitting in a cell today for going AWOL to get back to you. The temptation would have been too strong." He glanced at the clock on the dashboard. "It's been…four hours since I kissed you, and I'm already feeling Ally deprivation."

With a soft laugh, Alana caressed his nape. "Well, take an exit and let's get a room."

The truth was that Mack had intended to stop here all along and had made reservations for them at the five-star luxury hotel The Peabody. Mack hadn't wasted his time once Alana had committed to accompanying him on this trip. Fred's laptop had gotten a good workout as Mack researched and made plans. The hotel was a mere block away from historic Beale Street where the likes of Louis Armstrong and Muddy Waters had gained prominence, and B.B. King's Blues Club continued to flourish. One of the great attractions of the hotel was the Grand Lobby and the marble fountain, which was the playground to the world-famous Peabody Ducks.

Alana was delighted when she heard this was the place. "Oh, my goodness, I saw this on TV on one of the morning shows. What time do they come out?" she asked the reservationist, as they checked in.

"Eleven and five," the young woman replied, nodding toward the fountain. "If you wait another two minutes before going up to your room, you'll see them right over there."

Mack had to admit it was a cute scene, but better was Alana's reaction to their elegant room with the king-size bed and view of the city. "I knew there had to be an ounce or two of typical female in you," he drawled, as she gushed over the cream-and-coffee decor and the expansive marble bathroom. "After putting up with my blah bedroom, you deserve an atmosphere that does you justice."

Returning to him and wrapping her arms around his neck, she said, "What I'm most thrilled for is that *you* finally get a bed big enough to stretch out in."

But at the moment, sleep was the last thing on Mack's mind. With a thoroughly male smile, he easily tossed her onto the bed. "Let's find out," he replied.

An hour later, they dressed again and walked to Beale Street and had a drink at B.B.'s club. After listening to a few songs, they walked some more, finally returning to dress for dinner. They had reservations for eight-thirty downstairs at Chez Philippe. The opulent restaurant seemed to be designed like a Roman bath with descending tiers lined by glorious pillars that framed the various dining areas. Couches were nestled against walls, huge pots of palms added more privacy, and every table was set with continental elegance.

Mack had whistled as Alana emerged from the bathroom dressed in a simple black silk sheath that showed off her slim but toned rider's figure. He also enjoyed watching heads turn as he followed her to their table, pride testing the buttons on his silk dress shirt and gray suit jacket. He'd been doing some shopping; after all, he was a man on a mission.

He was also the former kid who, at sunrise on the morning of his eighteenth birthday, had stood waiting at an L.A. marine recruiting office until someone came to unlock the doors. He had handed them his birth certificate and high school diploma and said, "Get me the hell out of here." Having survived three wars and served his twenty years—a feat that surprised even him—he watched Alana be seated by the admiring maître d'. As with his soldiering, Mack was reinventing himself to be worthy. But this time he wasn't doing it for a corps, it was all for her.

"The wine steward will be here momentarily with your champagne, Mr. Graves," the maître d' said, his manner solicitous, as he presented their menus with a flourish. "I hope you will enjoy your evening."

Mack murmured his thanks a second before he felt Alana's fingers bite into his thigh under the table's two linen tablecloths. "We just drank some rum-drenched peach thingy, and haven't eaten since breakfast. *Champagne?* You'll have me humiliating you by falling out of this chair before our entrées even arrive."

"Which one? They happen to serve seven courses with their seasonal special dinners." He showed her in the menu.

Alana tried to keep from laughing, but failed. Mack realized her underestimation of what lay before her was so amusing to her, she had to dab tears from the corners of her eyes. By the time she recovered, their champagne arrived.

Once it was served, Mack lifted his glass to hers. "I hope you're still having this much fun by the time we're headed home."

After the crystal-clear musical sound, and the first taste of the bubbling wine, she put down her glass. Her expression grew a bit anxious. "Is this where you tell me the truth about what we're walking into at Quantico?"

"This has nothing to do with that. This is all about us."

"Oh." Pleasure transformed Alana's face into sheer bliss. "Sorry. Knee-jerk reaction."

Mack understood. That was another reason why he was doing this. "Then it's a good thing you took a break from being a cop when you did. That suspicious, expect-the-worst condition is trying to become chronic," he teased, reaching for her hand.

As soon as he spoke, he winced, realizing his mistake because her fear of bad news did, of course, go much further back. "I mean—"

Alana leaned over to kiss his smoothly shaved cheek. "I know. And you're right." She leaned closer yet to whisper in his ear. "But you have to admit that the idea of being frisked by me in the elevator on our way back to our room has a certain appeal."

It definitely did. In fact, the image stayed with Mack well past the Wild Salmon Gravlax Terrine with Goat Cheese, even to the Neda Farms Strip Loin, Haricots Verts, Potato Gratin, Roast Garlic and Juniper Berry Sauce.

"Can we walk again?" Alana asked, as they exited the restaurant only minutes before their usual closing time. "I feel as though I ate a bite of everything in the kitchen. Thank goodness French chefs grasp the wisdom in portioning." She sighed with pleasure. "That *was* blue-cheese grits, right? With the squab? God love the Europeans. We should ship them all the hominy south of the Mason-Dixon, and challenge them to get creative. I'll bet it would inspire the next blockbuster fast-food chain."

Enjoying her playfulness, Mack slipped his fingers through hers. "My surprise was the haricots verts. Who knew *haricot* means 'bean,' and *vert* means 'green'?"

"Ah," she said, wagging the index finger of the hand that held her clutch purse. "*Slender* green beans, not our chubby American ones." She chuckled softly. "That was wonderful."

Thinking the same, Mack led her toward the lobby doors. "Peabody Place is right next door. Shops, restaurants, clubs—" he glanced down at her strapless shoes "—nothing too far or difficult for you to handle in those sexy things."

"Sounds good."

But they'd barely made it a few hundred feet into the area, when the noise and crowds had Alana stopping and drawing him back. "It does look like fun...for someone else. You know what I think sounds like us?"

The open invitation in her eyes sent Mack's heart skipping a beat. "You have my undivided attention."

"To finish a perfect day, we could go back to our beautiful room, and get comfortable, and you could stretch out on that lovely bed while I give you a massage so that tomorrow morning when you get into the car, it won't feel as though you already marched ten miles."

Lifting their joined hands to his lips, he kissed her knuckles. "I am blessed among men."

Mack was a little disappointed that they made it up

the elevator without him getting frisked, but then they hadn't been alone in the car, either. However, Alana seemed intent on making that up to him.

Once in their room, while she made short work of slipping out of her heels and sliding out the combs that had held back her hair to expose her elegant neck, he leaned against the door to watch her. It was becoming one of his favorite pastimes. She didn't fuss. She could be ready to head out the door in five minutes if you asked it of her, but she still ended up looking like she'd spent two hours perfecting the results.

Her gaze lifted to his in the mirror, as she removed the diamond studs that she'd told him had been her mother's. With her lips curving, she crossed back to him and slowly unknotted his tie. "This isn't going to come off by itself."

"I got busy."

"You could make a girl shy when you stare at her like that."

"Like what? As though she's the only woman he ever wants to look at again?"

"Yeah." She went up on tiptoe and kissed him, in the process pulling the long band of red silk from around his neck. Laying it on the armchair beside them, she helped him out of his coat. "Confession time," she said, returning to him to remove his belt. "I'm the only female in my high school class who's never married. Okay, so there were only thirty-three of us in a class of fifty-nine...and one doesn't count because she died of a drug overdose in college, and another is serving life plus thirty for something we don't need to get into. The point is that I didn't see sex as anything more than it was until you. You make me feel very...special."

"Because you are."

With a beatific smile, and a kiss on his chin, she carried his things to the closet where she hung everything, unzipped her dress and hung it up, too. Wearing only black-lace-over-nude-silk panties and bra, she returned again, this time to take his hand and lead him to the bed. There, she urged him to sit, then knelt to remove his shoes and socks.

"I didn't speak for over a year after the crash," she continued quietly, as she worked. "Duke thought it would help to force me to go back to school. Until then I'd been doing assignments at home. The kids were nice at first, but then when their ancillary expectations weren't met, they treated me like a freak...until one day a classmate pushed me because I'd sat at the desk nearest the door, which was where she'd wanted to sit. That was the one thing we had in common—both of us couldn't wait to get out of class.

"It wasn't much of a push," she said with a slight shrug. "But I was pretty scrawny at that point, and I fell into the desk beside mine, which ultimately caused more time out of school because that's how I got this." She indicated the faint scar over her left eyebrow.

"Tough classmate. What did you do?" Mack asked.

"I got up and knocked her onto her butt using a little self-defense technique that my brother had taught me—and proceeded to call her every bad word I knew. Granted, that wasn't all that much at the ripe age of thirteen in Oak Grove, Texas, but it was something to behold from the silent girl who hadn't wanted to say a word for all that time."

Wishing he'd been there to protect her and help her, Mack drawled, "So that explains the low crime rate in town. You scared everyone into behaving. And here I thought it was mostly Big Duke's scowl."

With a brief laugh, Alana replied, "Yeah, I was becoming an angry little kid, and not even a big bully like that classmate could intimidate me. Would you believe she's now the high school principal?" As Mack uttered a brief choking sound, she went to work unbuttoning his shirt.

"The reason I brought up all of that," she continued mildly, "is to make you understand how much I mean it when I say that I know I can still be trying, and to thank you for being patient…and wise…and a gentleman, as much as you are a sweetheart, gyrene."

Stopping her as she started on his cuffs, Mack knew there was something he had to do now that couldn't wait any longer. He eased by her to get to his suitcase on the valet stand in the closet. When he returned, he urged her to sit beside him on the bed. "You can't be on your knees for this. Neither of us should, since I see us as more than a team or partnership. I see us…as one."

Opening his hand, he exposed a small velvet box. At first, he didn't think Alana was reacting. But then he saw her clasped hands tighten in her lap.

"What have you done?"

"What I knew I was going to do since watching you carry off a poisonous snake one night as though it was merely a lost frog trying to find its way back to the creek," he told her. "Do you think sharing what a stubborn but hurting little kid you were was going to stop me from loving you?" He opened the box to expose the solitaire he'd spent the most nerve-racking hour of his life choosing.

"I meant to offer this to you on the morning we headed for the ceremony," he continued. "To give us both something better to focus on. But the one thing I understand, given each of our journeys, is that life is suddenly going to be too damned short from here on, now that we've found each other. I don't know how much grace we'll be given, but waiting two more days to see you wearing this is two too many. So is getting to tell you that I love you."

Alana wrapped her arms around him. "Mack," she whispered. "You're the best thing that's ever happened to me."

Hearing the tears in her voice and feeling a rawness in his throat, Mack took the ring from its slot to slip it on her finger. He'd had to guess on the size, and didn't breathe until they discovered that it fit her perfectly.

"I can't believe this." She stared at the ring only to send him a helpless look. "It's too fine. When will it be safe to wear it? My hands are always in something."

"At least try to get used to using your *other* hand to feed Tanker his apples and carrots."

Laughingly agreeing, Alana's expression gentled. "You know this isn't necessary, don't you? As far as I'm concerned, things are perfect the way they are."

Mack purposely misunderstood and arched one eyebrow skeptically. "With half of your clothes at Last Call and the other half at Pretty Pines? I don't think so." Seeing her battle temptation and doubt in herself, he drew in a deep breath for the rest of his speech.

"I was a soldier for twenty years, Ally, and I swear I already know and understand you better than I ever did most of the guys I served with, even though I considered them some my best friends. What's more, you did for my father what my own mother couldn't, wouldn't do. I found and read his personal journals, too, sweetheart. The ones you tucked away in the attic."

Alana looked torn. "I didn't know whether to burn them or what, but they also showed he was a good man with a big heart, and you needed a chance to see that."

"He evolved into that because you gave him what love you could, despite the pain that you were struggling with. Those journals are practically love sonnets from a man who'd learned late what was worth cherishing. I don't intend to make that mistake. Marry me."

"Yes, Mack," she said, going into his arms again. "Yes and yes!"

"One more thing," he said, nuzzling her ear. "Stop taking those damned pills. Have my baby."

Chapter Nine

"Are you okay?"

Alana stood outside the bathroom door, certain that Mack had to be staring into the mirror and convincing himself to get today over with. They were in the apartment he'd swiftly packed up and left almost a month ago. But they hadn't spent the night here. When they'd arrived yesterday, he'd looked around and immediately ushered her out to get a room at a nice hotel a few miles away. They'd returned here this morning two hours before they were due at Quantico for him to get into his dress uniform.

Mack had shared that he hadn't put it on in almost a year. She hoped he wasn't concerned about the fit—he looked in perfect shape now to her—but after being wounded, his weight could still be under what he'd weighed when he first got it. She had to admit, she was eager to see him in it at least once before he packed it away for good.

Struggling to remain patient, Alana clasped her hands and her gaze settled on her ring which, as usual, managed to put a lump in her throat. They had much to be grateful for, including the commandant's and navy secretary's forgiveness over Mack's original rejection of this great recognition. He'd had a meeting with senior officials on base yesterday and, afterward, he'd assured her that they had made him understand that while his feelings of being undeserving were respected, he didn't fully grasp how tribute and ceremony were also necessary for those who would follow him in the corps. It would also honor and comfort the families of his fallen comrades. Mack told Alana that he continued to have his own opinion of that, but he had been pragmatic in the presence of his superiors.

If it gets us back to Texas for all of our tomorrows, he'd told her later, *I can give them their day.*

"Be right out," he called, in reply to Alana's concerned query.

Returning to her pacing, she hugged herself as she thought about him living here between deployments. She'd taken one look at the one-bedroom apartment and said to him, "And you thought Last Call needed work?"

Mack had unabashedly agreed that the place had been like a "holding pen" until his next orders were cut. Barren, impersonal, there was no danger that it would be missed while sleeping in a tent in a desert or camping under a tree while hiking to Texas. Yesterday he'd also gone to the complex's manager's office to notify them that he was forfeiting his deposit—he still had two months on his lease—and was moving out today. After notifying the furniture rental place as well, he and Alana had gone to buy boxes for his few remaining personal things to load into the car as soon as the ceremony was over.

Now if only we can get through that.

When he opened the door, Alana broke into a wondrous smile. Dear Lord, she thought, feeling both attraction and awe. He was magnificent in his dress uniform with all his previously earned medals and ribbons on his chest, and his hat and gloves in his hands.

"Look at you, Gunnery Sergeant Mackenzie Graves," she whispered. "I thought you were impressive in your civilian clothes." She stepped forward to cup his smooth-shaven cheeks and touched her lips to his. "You take my breath away."

And he did. He was also a different person, she realized. This was the warrior she'd had glimpses of since finding him along that flood-swollen creek. The discipline was back, the compartmentalizing, the shutting down of emotions. That, she didn't care for at all. In fact, it frightened her.

"Where's my Mack, sir?" she whispered. "I let him go in there a half hour ago, and he hasn't come out."

"I'm here, sweetheart," he said, his arms possessive, even as his kiss was gentle. "I'm just…"

"On the clock?" she offered.

He managed a crooked smile. "Something like that. For the last time." He stepped back to admire her. "But

I'm still the guy whose heart all but stops whenever he looks at you."

Alana had bought the navy blue wraparound dress that accentuated her trim figure with him in mind. The long-sleeved, knee-length dress would suit propriety, and so would her hair in a soft bun at her nape.

"Officer Anders in a dress would cause traffic accidents in Oak Grove."

"If I wore a dress back home, I'd never be taken seriously again. This is all for you."

Mack slipped his arms around her waist to bring her hip-to-hip against him. "Happy birthday to me."

"Remind me of the protocol, so I don't embarrass you?" she asked, her voice husky.

"We'll be received in a private room. You get compliments, I get my last butt chewing. Then you'll be escorted to your seat in the front row. I hear there will be press coverage, after all. I'm sorry. Just keep reading the printed program if it starts to get to you. But they do try to make it pretty easy on family and guests. I'm the shark bait."

Alana ached for him. "They'll read the citation?"

He sighed. "Yeah, after the secretary says a few words. Don't misunderstand if I don't look at you during that part."

"Of course not. I know it's not going to be easy."

It wasn't.

Just over two hours later, Alana watched Mack stand on the stage with assorted military and elected dignitaries, and watched the man she loved struggle to maintain his composure as he was extolled repeatedly. They read that he and his platoon had been in a remote location in Afghanistan about to withdraw after a successful mission, when they were suddenly ambushed.

In the end the entire platoon was removed from the field of battle. Mack pulled out four of his men himself. Not one of them escaped without being wounded, but only Mack survived those injuries.

Mack stood at attention for the reading of the names of the fallen.

Then the medal was presented and pinned on him.

Alana's heart wrenched repeatedly for him. She understood entirely why this was a psychological, as well as an emotional, injustice, if not an assault. Nevertheless, she schooled her emotions and kept her gaze on him to mentally will him to get through it. That was all that mattered, although from her new perspective, he'd entirely earned this recognition.

At the same time, she thought it was a farce to speak of "closure." The two others besides Mack, who had still been alive when rescued, only lived long enough to know family members were with them. Alana could accept that those were precious gifts in a way, and yet they were nothing close to what she knew Mack believed he'd owed his men. His friends.

After the ceremony was over, she waited as he was embraced, and his back slapped, and his hand was grasped by too many to count—dignitaries, military personnel, families of the fallen.

Finally, he came to her and just wrapped his arms

around her. She almost wept at the subtle trembling coming from deep inside his strong body.

"I'm here. What do you want to do?" she asked him. "I'll get you to the car right now if you want me to."

He hugged her tighter. "If only. But we have to do the rest. There's a little luncheon reception."

Alana all but gasped. "How do they expect you to swallow one bite after all that?"

He uttered a low sound of agreement. "But I would like to introduce you to a few people."

Determined to do him proud, Alana took his arm and lifted her chin. "It would be a privilege."

It was only as they exited the base that Mack finally felt the strain leave his body. It hadn't been the worst experience in his life; that had happened on that gray day a half world away, and more recently in a small Texas town during a waning moon when he thought newfound love would be stolen from him. But he certainly didn't intend to put himself or Ally through anything like it again.

"So now we get to go change and pack up this pretty stagecoach?" she asked, breaking into his thoughts.

Mack knew what she was doing as she teased and placed her hand on his thigh. She was also gauging his tension level.

"We do," he replied, taking comfort in feeling her ring press against his palm as he covered her hand with his. He'd never been more grateful or proud of her demeanor throughout that whole stressful event. She had marine qualities herself—even the secretary of the navy shared his admiration and approval after being introduced to her.

"How far do you think we can get from here by sunset?" Alana asked.

His humor returning, Mack drawled, "Well, I thought we could make D.C. before evening traffic creates one big parking lot."

Gasping, Alana straightened in her seat. "Mack, no! We have to go *there?*"

He couldn't do it. Shaking his head, he reassured her. "I take it that you don't want a tour of the White House?"

"Maybe another time."

She'd all but said those words through gritted teeth. He was going to marry a homebody, and that was exactly what he wanted. "I did have one idea. Why don't we detour a bit and head back home through Kentucky, so you can see their horse country?"

"What do you know about Kentucky horse country?"

"I didn't always stay in that ugly apartment." Glancing over to intercept her look of surprise, he added, "Maybe we'll even pick up some house ideas."

"That sounds…interesting," Alana allowed, starting to look bemused. "Especially if we could also find a hotel that has a balcony."

"Because?"

"We're about to have our one month anniversary."

"I knew that. I was wondering if you remembered." Of course Mack knew she did.

"We may not have another blue moon to celebrate

for a while, but an almost-full moon seems perfect in its own way, doesn't it?"

"You and moonlight definitely go together."

Epilogue

Thanksgiving Day

"It's time for a toast."

Alana watched her uncle rise with his wineglass in hand. As always, his presence had its effect on things, and everyone around the table grew respectfully silent. They'd just said grace, and Sam Carlyle had carved the turkey with Bunny serving the succulent slices to everyone else. In between, Mack was answering Bunny's son's questions about the aircraft carriers he'd sailed on, and Eberardo was looking very much in love and proud as his fiancée, Maria, assisted getting the side dishes passed around the table.

It was Mack and Alana's first Thanksgiving as a married couple. A week after returning to Texas, they'd collected Duke and Bunny and had married in a judge's chambers in Quitman, Texas, Wood County's county seat. Neither of them had wanted anything more complicated or fussy. They were beginning their life together on their terms, and today was another step in that direction.

Wanting to start their own traditions, they'd decided to bring together the people they loved, and the people finding their own love. That was a challenge considering that they were also building a new house just about where the gate was that divided Last Call from Pretty Pines—one day to be removed as both properties joined, just as Mack and Alana were joining their lives.

Duke tapped his dessert spoon against his glass of red wine, even though everyone waited expectantly. "I always wanted to do that," he said with an impish smile.

Alana patted his back as the others laughed. "You have the floor, Chief. Go!"

With his chest thrusting, he beamed at her. "Well, isn't this something? This time last year, Ally and I were popping frozen dinners into the microwave, and today we have a scene straight out of *Eat, Pray, Love*."

Alana exchanged shocked looks with Bunny. "What do you know about *Eat, Pray, Love*?"

"I hate to tell you this, my girl, but you didn't invent insomnia."

"Especially if the best you could do was TV dinners," Sam piped in.

Duke gave him a sheepish look. "You may have something there." Then he raised his glass higher. "So then, Sam...thank you for this excellent wine and for keeping the ladies straight in the kitchen. Barbara, may you and Sam here continue to stir up magic—not all of it in the kitchen. Thank you, and welcome, lovely Maria, for agreeing to put up with Eberardo, here. Thank you, Chris, because I've never seen you in my station," he added to Bunny's son. "And most of all to the newly-weds—" Duke teared up. "I may have lost a fine officer, but my niece has gained a man truly worthy of her. That is what I'm grateful for this Thanksgiving."

Applause and cheers filled the crowded room, and Alana kissed her uncle's cheek as soon as he resumed his seat. Then the serious eating commenced. Sam had, indeed, been integral in helping to create their feast. He was gifted in more than gardening, and while Barbara's son, Chris, seemed more intrigued with Mack than Sam, the two got along well enough. As for Barbara Jayne, she was positively glowing. She, too, was giving up her night-shift-dispatcher job at Sam's request. She wasn't yet sold on gardening as much as he was, but when they were in the kitchen together, the results were worthy of heavenly choruses.

As for Eberardo and Maria, things looked promising. Alana thought there was no doubt that Maria was in love with Eberardo. But having worked so hard to make something of herself to where she was a respected nurse at the local hospital, she hadn't been willing to sell herself short. However, after Mack told Eberardo that when they moved into the new house, he could purchase this house and make it the foreman's residence in an owner-financed agreement, Maria finally let her head yield to what her heart wanted, and she accepted Eberardo's proposal.

Antonio had been invited as well, but he was in a relationship, too, and he had been expected at his girl-friend's family home. It would appear that the new house would be done just in time for Eberardo's and Antonio's expanding families.

"You're quiet," Mack said, reaching under the table to touch her thigh. "Everything okay?"

"Wonderful. I'm just taking in all of this."

"It was a good idea you had." When she slid his hand into his, he squeezed it gently. "The Peabody would be hard-pressed to top Sam's turkey."

"Have you tasted this yet?" Alana fed him a bite of the stuffing that was a feast of its own, being a mixture of sausage, fruit, herbs and wild rice.

Moaning his appreciation, Mack glanced across the table. "Where's the bowl with the stuffing? Eberardo, I see you hiding it behind the biscuit basket. Hand it over, buddy."

The conversation stayed lighthearted. Even so, Chris vanished first to get to the TV for the traditional Thanksgiving Day Cowboys football game, while everyone else decided clearing the table and taking a walk would be smarter before dessert was served. Alana used that opportunity to excuse herself and Mack to head to the cemetery for a few minutes.

She wrapped three white roses and one red from the centerpiece she'd had made for their table and held them as Mack drove them the short distance into town.

She was grateful that Mack had been agreeable to her idea, and Alana watched him with a new sense of serenity.

"What?" he asked, catching on to her preoccupation.

"Just living in the moment."

"It's a good day," he said. "It'll be a better one when everyone goes home."

Alana reached over to caress his cheek. "I lucked out in the romantic man department."

"You make it easy, my love."

Once Mack parked, he came around to open Alana's door and kept her hand resting on his arm as they crossed to the gravesite where her parents and Chase were buried. As always, Alana gazed at the gray marble and felt the wave of emotion that was as endless as an ocean's tides. But today there was also new joy.

As she placed the white roses on the monuments, she said, "Hi Mom, Dad, Chase. It's us. We couldn't leave you out on Thanksgiving. Won't miss the kick-off, Chase. But I wanted you to be part of this as I tell Mack something."

She turned to her husband. "What was in my glass wasn't wine, it was cranberry juice. Hiding that from the girls *and* you was an accomplishment, let me tell you." At his perplexed look, she asked, "Are you the last man on the planet who doesn't know why a woman does that? I'm pregnant, darling."

Without a word, Mack folded her into his arms. "I should have known. You do nothing like anyone else does. Ally...sweetheart." He took a sustaining breath. "When?"

"Probably some hours after the ceremony in the justice of the peace's office."

Mack looked at the sky and laughed. Then, touching

his forehead to hers, he gazed into her eyes and asked, "When will the baby get here?"

"Okay, smarty. Have your fun," she purred. "June. You *know* the day."

"Yes, ma'am, I do. It was the best out of the other 365." He followed that with a kiss that left her unable to walk. Fortunately Mack's strong arm was now determinedly wrapped around her waist.

Moving over to Fred's grave, Mack placed the red rose there. "Well, sir, did you hear that?" He immediately drew Alana into his arms again and buried his face in her hair. "How can I tell you how happy and blessed I feel?"

"It's the same for me. I love you so, Mack."

"I'm going to take my time absorbing that—*and you*—like the world's most decadent dessert, and maybe in thirty or forty years, I'll figure out why."

Of course he knew why. She knew why. It was that simple, and that complicated and wonderful. Alana took hold of his hand and drew it to her still-flat tummy. "Take me home, Daddy. Mama needs dessert."

* * * * *

COMING NEXT MONTH from Harlequin
Special Edition®
AVAILABLE JUNE 19, 2012

#2197 THE LAST SINGLE MAVERICK
Montana Mavericks: Back in the Saddle
Christine Rimmer
Steadfastly single cowboy Jason Traub asks Jocelyn Bennings to accompany him to his family reunion to avoid any blind dates his family has planned for him. Little does he know that she's a runaway bride—and that he's about to lose his heart to her!

#2198 THE PRINCESS AND THE OUTLAW
Royal Babies
Leanne Banks
Princess Pippa Devereaux has never defied her family except when it comes to Nic Lafitte. But their feuding families won't be enough to keep these star-crossed lovers apart.

#2199 HIS TEXAS BABY
Men of the West
Stella Bagwell
The relationship of rival horse breeders Kitty Cartwright and Liam Donovan takes a whole new turn when an unplanned pregnancy leads to an unplanned romance.

#2200 A MARRIAGE WORTH FIGHTING FOR
McKinley Medics
Lilian Darcy
The last thing Alicia McKinley expects when she leaves her husband, MJ, is for him to put up a fight for their marriage. What surprises her even more is that she starts falling back in love with him.

#2201 THE CEO'S UNEXPECTED PROPOSAL
Reunion Brides
Karen Rose Smith
High school crushes Dawson Barrett and Mikala Conti are reunited when Dawson asks her to help his traumatized son recover from an accident. When sparks fly and a baby on the way complicates things even more, can this couple make it work?

#2202 LITTLE MATCHMAKERS
Jennifer Greene
Being a single parent is hard, but Garnet Cottrell and Tucker MacKinnon have come up with a "kid-swapping" plan to help give their boys a more well-rounded upbringing. But unbeknownst to their parents the boys have a matchmaking plan of their own.

You can find more information on upcoming Harlequin® titles, free excerpts and more at www.HarlequinInsideRomance.com.   HSECNM0612

REQUEST YOUR FREE BOOKS!

2 FREE NOVELS PLUS 2 FREE GIFTS!

❧ Harlequin®

SPECIAL EDITION

Life, Love & Family

The Bowman siblings have avoided Christmas ever since a family tragedy took the lives of their parents during the holiday years ago. But twins Trace and Taft Bowman have gotten past their grief, courtesy of the new women in their lives. Is it sister Caidy's turn to find love—perhaps with the new veterinarian in town?

Read on for an excerpt from
A COLD CREEK NOEL by USA TODAY
bestselling author RaeAnne Thayne, next in her ongoing series THE COWBOYS OF COLD CREEK

***

"For what it's worth, I think the guys around here are crazy. Even if you did grow up with them."

He might have left things at that, safe and uncomplicated, except his eyes suddenly shifted to her mouth and he didn't miss the flare of heat in her gaze. He swore under his breath, already regretting what he seemed to have no power to resist, and then he reached for her.

As his mouth settled over hers, warm and firm and tasting of cocoa, Caidy couldn't quite believe this was happening.

She was being kissed by the sexy new veterinarian, just a day after thinking him rude and abrasive. For a long moment she was shocked into immobility, then heat began to seep through her frozen stupor. Oh. Oh, yes!

How long had it been since she had enjoyed a kiss and wanted more? She was astounded to realize she couldn't really remember. As his lips played over hers, she shifted her neck slightly for a better angle. Her insides seemed to give a collective shiver. Mmm. This was exactly what two people ought to be doing at 3:00 a.m. on a cold December day.

He made a low sound in his throat that danced down her spine, and she felt the hard strength of his arms slide around her, pulling her closer. In this moment, nothing else seemed to matter but Ben Caldwell and the wondrous sensations fluttering through her.

Still, this was crazy. Some tiny voice of self-preservation seemed to whisper through her. What was she doing? She had no business kissing someone she barely knew and wasn't even sure she liked yet.

Though it took every last ounce of strength, she managed to slide away from all that delicious heat and move a few inches away from him, trying desperately to catch her breath.

The distance she created between them seemed to drag Ben back to his senses. He stared at her, his eyes looking as dazed as she felt. "That was wrong. I don't know what I was thinking. Your dog is a patient and…I shouldn't have…"

She might have been offended by the dismay in his voice if not for the arousal in his eyes. But his hair was a little rumpled and he had the evening shadow of a beard and all she could think was *yum*.

***

Can Caidy and Ben put their collective pasts behind them and find a brilliant future together?

Find out in A COLD CREEK NOEL, coming in December 2012 from Harlequin Special Edition. And coming in 2013, also from Harlequin Special Edition, look for Ridge's story….

HSEEXP1212

**A brand-new Westmoreland novel
from *New York Times* bestselling author**

BRENDA JACKSON

Riley Westmoreland never mixes business with pleasure—until he meets his company's gorgeous new party planner. But when he gets Alpha Blake into bed, he realizes one night will never be enough. That's when her past threatens to end their affair. So Riley does what any Westmoreland male would do…he lets the fun begin.

ONE WINTER'S NIGHT

"Jackson's characters are…hot enough to burn the pages."
—*RT Book Reviews* on *Westmoreland's Way*

Available from Harlequin® Desire December 2012!

When legacy commands, these Greek royals must obey!

Discover a page-turning new Harlequin Presents®
duet from *USA TODAY* bestselling author

Maisey Yates

A ROYAL WORLD APART

Desperate to escape an arranged marriage, Princess
Evangelina has tried every trick in her little black book
to dodge her security guards. But where everyone else
has failed, will her new bodyguard bend her to his
will…and steal her heart?

Available November 13, 2012.

AT HIS MAJESTY'S REQUEST

Prince Stavros Drakos rules his country like his
business—with a will of iron! And when duty demands
an heir, this resolute bachelor will turn his sole
focus to the task….

But will he finally have met his match in a world-
renowned matchmaker?

Coming December 18, 2012,
wherever books are sold.

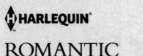

ROMANTIC
SUSPENSE

Get your heart racing this holiday season with double the pulse-pounding action.

Christmas Confidential

Featuring

Holiday Protector by **Marilyn Pappano**

Miri Duncan doesn't care that it's almost Christmas. She's got bigger worries on her mind. But surviving the trip to Georgia from Texas is going to be her biggest challenge. Days in a car with the man who broke her heart and helped send her to prison—private investigator Dean Montgomery.

A Chance Reunion by **Linda Conrad**

When the husband Elana Novak left behind five years ago shows up in her new California home she knows danger is coming her way. To protect the man she is quickly falling for Elana must convince private investigator Gage Chance that she is a different person. But Gage isn't about to let her walk away…even with the bad guys right on their heels.

Available December 2012 wherever books are sold!

www.Harlequin.com

HRS27801